BLEAKEST

EARTH ENDURES 3

BLEAKEST

JACQUELINE DRUGA

PRESS

Published by Vulpine Press in the United Kingdom in 2025

Cover by Vulpine Press

ISBN: 978-1-83919-626-3

www.vulpine-press.com

Also by Jacqueline Druga:

What we Become

Like many, Mackenzie Garret complains about the weather. It is the hottest summer anyone can remember. The high temperatures are out of control with no end in sight. Until it all changes.

Overnight, blue skies become gray, and the hot, humid weather turns to rain, then snow, then ice as the temperature plummets.

The entire northern half of the country is thrown into chaos as blow by blow, storm after storm, nature rips into the world, tearing it apart. Towns and cities are evacuated, and Mac and her family are forced to leave their world behind and face a treacherous journey south to safety.

Will they make it, or will they be left behind in this new, frozen world?

Omnicide

A town practically cut off from the rest of the country, Griffin is always the last to know about everything. Fax is the most reliable method of communication and the local newspaper is the main source of outside information.

When a freak car accident occurs on the outside of town, no one thinks much of it. That is until deer are found sick and covered in an unusual growth, and they lose contact with the next town.

Cut off and isolated from the rest of the world, Griffin is unaware of the threat growing outside the safety of their little town. One that could endanger their entire existence.

TALES OF THE LOST ARC

ARC-373
Day: 4208
Commander's Log Entry 4186

March 6

Another fight has broken out in the agricultural division. It damaged the pumps. I never would have imagined that we would fraction off as we did. Groups like countries. The children that are now adults are the most vocal about injustice.

What injustice.

We are above Earth, biding time, watching the slow destruction.

As commander I must make a decision. Stay for the Androski or land.

I decided to leave it to a vote.

The majority chooses.

The vote happens tonight.

Commander JV Arlington

ONE
THE SHIP

It wasn't the way it was supposed to happen. Nothing was.

For Commander Aldar Finch, growing up he never foresaw a dying world. One riddled with natural disasters, robots, AI all because of a blue planet making its way to Earth.

It would collide, it would stop, get into a rotation, and be a moon to Earth. But not before that blue planet caused a lot of damage. Damage that would kill billions.

When Earth realized the threat, they had a plan. Countries from all over built their own ARCs. A lottery would take place, and those chosen would abandon the dying Earth.

Those who remained would go to the small safe zones where survivability stood a chance.

Finch was put on a mission: find another Earth for the ARCs to go to.

It was called Project Noah, and he was commander of the Omni spacecraft.

Noah was inspired by a NOAA satellite that returned decades after being lost in space. It contained images of a lush and fertile planet.

A safe, new home had been found.

The Omni mission was conceived. It would go first, followed by the ARCs.

It seemed simple enough because even if it was hundreds of light years away, they had a way there, the same way the NOAA satellite arrived...

The wormhole Androski.

It opened every twenty-five years, and stayed open for a few months. Usually three.

The Omni would go through first, explore the new planet and return so the ARCs could start preparing for when the Androski opened again.

As Finch and his Omni crew would learn, the Androski wasn't a gateway to another galaxy, it was Einstein's theory proven correctly.

It was a portal in time, but a time machine with no controls, and it seemed to move whatever passed through it in the time intervals that matched the Androski emergence.

Twenty-five years.

When Finch and his crew landed on the Noah planet, they discovered it was Earth...one hundred and seventy-five years after they had left.

The two ships that left twenty-five years after the Omni were also there: the Robinson and the Genisis.

Finch wanted to try to go home, to get back to his time, Earth-0 as they called it now, and the only way to do that was to go through the Androski again.

Not many wanted to try because it was a coin toss on where they would go.

Sure, they could go home, back to Earth-0, but there was just as much of a chance they could land in another time.

And they did.

Finch, Nate, and Ray, from the Omni crew, were joined by Tucker and Sam of the LOLA mission.

They landed seventy-five years past Finch's time.

Information was gathered about what had happened to the world, but Earth-75 proved deadly and they left again. They'd gotten their hands on some sort of record. A first-person experience from an ARC that had landed in that time. Finch would read it, learn it, know it. Even if it didn't help all that much, it would hopefully give them insight into what happened on Earth-75.

Finch knew when they passed back through the Androski again, they'd gone back in time, farther back because the blue planet that threatened to bring extinction-level destruction to Earth wasn't there. It wasn't a moon.

It wasn't visible.

They were thrilled when the voices of NASA carried over their radio as they made an approach to Earth.

They'd done it.

They'd made it.

They were home.

They couldn't have been more wrong.

ARC-373
Day: 4209
Commander's Log Entry 4187

March 7

It is the dawn of a new era, and not one I agree with. But a vote has been taken and seventy-five percent of our crew and residents do not want to wait another five years for the Androski to open.

We will land.

We've charted a course for Colorado, somewhere in there.

I can see Earth. It has been my morning, evening, and night view for the last ten years while we have been in orbit. Now we return home. We have watched disaster sweep the world and seen explosions that could only be manmade weapons.

What has become of below, we will soon find out.

I have been unable to reach Earth for three years, but only my crew knows this. Morale is low enough for the passengers as it is.

The artificial sunlight isn't working for them.

For years it did.

I suppose I would like to feel the sun on my face like they do.

Is that possible?

A part of me wants to just leave after we land. Take a vehicle and go. But I know I can't. Once we land I must find a way for people to survive. We have the tools and equipment. Will we have the strength?

Commander JV Arlington

TWO
THE CREW VIEW

A part of Rey didn't believe it when she heard NASA on the radio.

Everyone cheered when NASA ground said, "This is Houston. We have you. Go ahead."

Having gotten to know Finch, Rey saw he contained his enthusiasm, holding up his hand to make everyone be quiet. He lifted the radio, and was ready to say something when the other voice came on.

"Yeah, uh Houston, are you seeing anything down there?"

"Sorry, Endeavor can you repeat what you mean?" Houston questioned.

Rey wondered if they could even hear Omni if they tried to reach out.

"The Endeavor?" Finch asked. "That was a space shuttle."

No way, Rey thought. No way. Finch had to be wrong.

"Roger that, Houston, do the Russians have anything up here? Over."

"That's a negative, Endeavor."

"Well, you guys are gonna are gonna think we're nuts, but…we're seeing a ship of unidentified origins."

Rey closed her eyes, a ship of unidentified origins. It was the Omni.

"Can you get us a visual, Endeavor," requested Houston.

"Roger that we'll try."

Tucker called out, "There. I see it. I see the Endeavor."

Sam replied, "They see us."

The Houston command spoke again. "We see it. It is not one of ours."

"We're gonna try to make contact with the craft," the other voice said.

"Roger that. It's a go but keep your distance until we identify it."

"Roger that."

There was silence for a second, then the voice returned. "This is an attempt to reach the unidentified craft. Do you copy?" Pause. "This Is Commander Ronald Grabe of the United States Airforce, flying STS-57, on the Endeavor. Do you read?"

Finch hurriedly turned to Rey. "You're a history teacher. When was the Endeavor, STS-57?"

Was he really asking her that, like she could pull that information out of her ass? "I...I...don't know." She shook her head. "I'm a teacher. I don't have a database that I can tap into that goes very far back."

"Shit," Tucker said then rushed to the computer set up by Nate. "We do. Sam and I brought it." His fingers tapped away on the keyboard.

The commander of the Endeavor repeated the call. "We are trying to make contact with the unknown craft, can you identify yourself. We are pulling closer and are not a threat."

Then suddenly Tucker rambled fast and excitedly, "Oh my God. Oh my God. Oh my God."

"What?" Finch asked.

Tucker's eyes widened. "I got it. Space Shuttle Endeavor. Mission STS-57, Commander Ronald Grabe...Finch, that mission launched June twenty-first," he said, "of 1993. We're in 1993."

Sam's voice was loud and shrill in his shock even though he processed it slightly when Finch pretty much outran the Endeavor. Sam was still in disbelief. "1993!" His voice cracked in a pre-pubescent way.

"Oh my God, oh my God," Tucker repeated.

Tucker and Sam were inventors, engineers, super intelligent men, yet they sounded like teenagers.

"It can't be right," said Sam.

"It is. It is."

"Oh my God."

"That's what I said."

"1993?"

Tucker nodded.

"Can it be wrong?"

Tucker shook his head. "The Androski works in twenty-five-year jumps."

Almost with a groan, Nate spoke up. He was still heavily medicated from his surgery and probably not processing their discovery. How could he? After all he had been disemboweled by the Riser robot and saved by Buster the medical bot with a surgical technique that had yet been explained to him. "So, wait, instead of going to the future, we went fifty years *before* the Omni Mission?"

Tucker threw up his hands. "None of us were even born yet."

"Except..." Sam tilted his head and everyone looked Finch.

"What?" Finch said. "I was like one."

"Do you think it would be bad if he met himself?" Rey asked.

Finch shook his head. "I won't meet myself because we won't be down there that long. We need to land, recharge the ship, and get back out. So that's like what? At most twenty-four hours. We need to find a safe spot to put her down." He turned his head to a mechanical sound and saw Buster the Med Robot making his way in. "Why is that thing in here?"

"I am concerned," said Buster. "All heartbeats except for Nate's have increased drastically."

Tucker told him, "That's because we are in 1993. We went back in time. We're in a bit of shock."

"1993," Buster said then paused a beat. "If it helps, in 1993 Massachusetts Eye and Ear clinicians pioneered the use of photodynamic therapy for neovascular macular degeneration."

Tucker squinched up his face. "Nah, yeah, it doesn't help, Buddy."

"What will help." Finch stood. "Is if someone, even that"—he pointed to Buster—"finds us a place to land. Somewhere out of sight and safe for long enough to recharge." Finch paused before leaving the cockpit. "And preferably, in a dream scenario, get us to Earth under the radar. We do not need to be found. Not in 1993."

"You okay?" Rey found Finch in the back medical bay area.

"Yeah, looking for an aspirin."

Rey snorted a laugh.

"And that's funny?"

"Sorry, just thinking if Buster heard you."

"How are you feeling?" Finch asked.

"Like I did an ab workout," Rey answered. "I can't believe he cloned my organs for Nate."

"I can't believe the size of the hole in Nate." After a grunt, Finch rubbed the top of his head. "We have to land."

"And we can't go back through?"

"Ideally, no." Finch shook his head. "What if we go back farther? What if we go back to 1968 or worse 1943?"

"But we can try to jump again."

"We can," Finch replied. "But we'll use all of our power and we may not have a choice where we land. Right now, we do. We can stay out here for another hour; I know it doesn't sound like much, but an hour to figure out what we do. Then we land, recharge, and we blast back through the Androski."

"Recharging will give us time to read that logbook."

"True. But we have to face something, Rey."

"What's that?"

"That hole is going to close, eventually, and we'll be stuck where we land."

"We can jump a bunch of times as long as we recharge, right. Jump until the Androski closes."

Finch nodded. "I want to go home. Back to our time or even twenty-five years after we left. I don't care. I know where we can go to be safe from disasters and warn people. Our entire mission was to save humanity. We've failed unless we get home."

"They made a show about us." Rey smiled. "That's not failure. That's kind of cool. Tucker was a huge fan. And humanity survived, we saw that. Just not as we hoped."

"Those ARCs have to get off the ground. I still have to finish reading those entries in the logbook from the ARC. They'll help us warn people."

"We're supposed to read them together," Rey said.

"I know."

"We know the ARCs got off the ground. We know what happened on Earth-75. Whoever jumped and changed time, causing the robots or Risers as they were called, landed in our time. That's Sam's guess."

"Mine, too," Finch said. "And the only saving grace is that they were able to say humanity did make it."

"I don't think they needed them or us to tell them that," Rey said. "We were afraid of the Big Blue. It was causing so much destruction. I think we just needed to know it wasn't the end."

"Wasn't it." Finch sighed out. "Right now, we need to land. We need to not get shot down doing so. It works in our favor that there wasn't really any internet in 1993, and technology isn't what we have now. I mean, we outran the shuttle by a long shot. But it's still a modern society, how are we going to slip by?"

"We got the top two minds and Buster on it, I'm sure they'll find a way."

"Find a location and a way to slip under the radar in an hour?" Finch shook his head. "I doubt that."

"Hey guys." Tucker poked his head into the med bay. "Come on up front. We found a way."

ARC-373
Day: 4211
Commander's Log Entry 4188

March 9

The entries will be sparce. Upon entry we were shot down.
Some sort of weapon I have never seen, like a light from the
ground.
    We tried radio contact.
    Nothing.
    We suffered losses both in the attack and the emergency
landing.
    Must assess.

Commander JV Arlington

THREE
THE WAY

The doorway to the workroom where Sam and Tucker had been working was closed. It struck Finch as odd. The three of them plus a robot crammed into that small area at some point.

Tucker was overexcited, rubbing his hands together as he stood before the closed door. "You guys ready?"

"Yes." Finch nodded.

"I'm so excited this reminds me of Season Two, Episode Nine when you guys were stuck in the gravitational pull of the hostile alien planet. Trying to find a way not to go down there, but not really having a choice. I thought for sure you were gonna die in that episode, Finch."

"Tucker," Finch said.

"Yeah?"

"That wasn't us. It was a show. Open the door."

"Okay." Tucker knocked on the door. "You guys ready?"

"Yep," Sam hollered.

"I, too, am ready," replied Buster.

"Wait until you see," Tucker said. "Or not."

"Tucker, open the damn door."

"Okay." Tucker did. "We can head down now. Not only did we find a great place to land, we can get there unseen."

"Sort of," Sam added. "We have a window where we can't be seen."

"How?" Finch asked and turned left to right. The room was small. "Where's Buster?"

"Here," Buster spoke up but wasn't seen.

"That's how." Sam pointed out.

Buster reappeared and Finch jumped a little. "What the hell?"

Rey lifted her hand. "I'm sorry if this is a dumb question, but how is making Buster invisible helping us?"

Finch answered, "They're using his tech."

A snap of his finger and Sam pointed. "Bingo."

"A little tech," Tucker said, "that was built into Buster as protection. We just need to tweak it, which we can."

"And it can be done?" asked Finch.

Sam nodded. "Yep. But there are a couple of problems. One, it will drain a lot of power from both Buster and the ship. Both will need to recharge. The other problem is, with a fully charged ship we get a good two hours of invisibility, with maybe a glitch of us here and there. But we're not going in with that much, so I am figuring fifteen minutes, tops."

"All we need," Finch said, "is to land, be safe, and recharge. Twenty-four hours. Who cares if we're not invisible when we leave, right?" Finch turned his head when he heard the groan from Rey. "What? What is wrong?"

"You have never seen *Planet of the Apes*, have you?" she asked.

"That's a hundred years before my time," said Finch.

"I saw it," Tucker added. "Then again that was after you brought it up in Season Three, episode—"

"Tucker." Finch cut him off. "Rey, why are you bringing up *Planet of the Apes*?"

"Because, as much as we want to believe they won't see us, at some point they'll catch us coming in and have a direction. If they come for us, we must, and I mean absolutely must, make the ship invisible or we'll be as bad as the Genesis Bandits. The ones who changed time."

"That's not going to happen if we find an out-of-the-way location. And what does that have to do with *Planet of the Apes*?"

Rey replied, "When the apes came from the future and landed in 1972 people found them, tried to kill them, and it jumped the entire ape timeline by thousands of years."

Sam muttered out, "The Genesis Bandits. They already jumped the timeline."

Finch wagged a finger. "But they haven't done it yet. Not in 1993. That…that we know of. Plus, if I remember correctly there were eight, I mean, eight other ships from other countries going through the Androski. They could be skipping about time like us and made, or will make, the change. It's confusing."

Rey exhaled. "I totally forgot about all the other ships."

"We all did," said Finch. "Okay, so what is the landing plan?"

Sam turned his chair to the computer. "Nothing we can do about breaking through the atmosphere, they'll spot us. But if we time this right, we break through, drop below radar, then go invisible somewhere around west Texas and at a good speed we can stay invisible until we land in Nevada."

"Which means," Tucker added, "yeah, they'll see us come in, but after Texas they won't know where we've gone."

"We land," Sam said, "and charge up. In fact, we can move the charging panels outside and keep the craft in the hanger. Which is big enough. It's perfect."

"Where?" Finch asked. "Where is this place?"

"Near Warm Springs, Nevada, in the desert," Sam said. "It was built in 1968 by the Department of Atomic Energy and closed in 1981."

"Are you sure it's still standing?" Finch asked.

"Yes."

"And abandoned?"

"Sort of."

"What?" Finch questioned.

"According to the intel I have, there are three people who live there and work there at all times. A guard, a scientist, and maintenance person."

Finch tossed up his hand. "Okay, so they won't see us land? Right?"

"See us?" Sam shook his head. "No. Hear us? Yes. So we have two choices."

Tucker nodded and stated, "We can kill them…"

Both Finch and Rey blasted, "What?"

"Or…" Tucker held his hand out to Buster. "We sedate them. Buster even has a medication that will make them forget. However, he'll need to recharge for at least two hours before he can be a medical bot, meaning he has to charge before he can give the injection."

"Can we sedate them?" Finch asked.

"Yes. Maybe they won't be there," Tucker said. "It's possible the three people working thing is a deterrent for sightseers. But if they see anything or look for us, we can knock them out.'

"I say kill them," Rey said. When she saw the reactions, she laughed. "I'm joking. Oh my God."

"Ha!" Tucker laughed. "You pulled that same joke in Season Two…"

"Tucker!" Finch snapped. "Stop. Alright. Get me the coordinates and the timing, I'll set a course and inform Nate." He stepped back to the door. "What is this base called?"

"Basecamp," answered Sam.

"Basecamp?" Finch asked. "Just basecamp."

"Well, Secret Basecamp if you want to be official," Sam said. "It was said they had aliens and stuff there."

Tucker laughed.

"Don't." Finch pointed. "No Episode references please."

"What if we've been here before?" Rey said. "Not yet, but we jump through and end up in the sixties. What if we're the aliens?"

On that, Finch walked out.

FOUR
HOUSTON, WE HAVE A PROBLEM

The moment he got the call saying, "They're back," Martin Weissman, director of NASA, forewent his Dunkaroos and ran straight to the control room. He made it there in less than three minutes, impressive for a man waiting on a hip replacement.

It was supposed to be a simple ten-day mission. The Endeavor was on course and time to land in Florida with Houston taking controls.

But an hour earlier, Commander Grabe reported to CAPCOM that he'd spotted a craft that wasn't recognizable. But as Grabe approached, he also reported the craft took off back into space at an incredible high rate of speed.

That was that.

Endeavor continued the approach and Martin took a brief lunch, making calls to the Pentagon and the Air Force to see if they could identify the craft.

Six minutes before he got the "They're back" message, he was assured no one else was up there. That was when Martin ran.

"What?" Martin was out of breath when he entered the control room. "What's going on?"

His chief control officer, Gene Hayward, pointed to the speakers then asked the CAPCOM officer in charge of communicating with the shuttle to get them to repeat.

"Endeavor, can you repeat."

"It just passed us, the same craft."

Gene then pointed to the radar. "We see it. We got it."

"Is that headed toward us?" Martin asked.

"Right toward the atmosphere. Should be entering in about six minutes."

"Jesus, how fast?"

"It's taking everything Endeavor has to keep up."

Gene took over the communications. "Endeavor, this is FD Hayward. We're tracking it now. We have it on our radar. Do you have eyes on the prize?"

"We do. Quickly losing visual," reported Commander Grabe.

"Can you describe it?"

"NASA...this is going to sound insane."

Martin closed his eyes, rubbing the corners, expecting to hear it was a flying saucer or something of that nature.

"But," Grabe continued, "it looks like a super-size shuttle."

Martin stopped rubbing his eyes and looked up.

"And it has a flag on it. NASA, it's an American flag."

"Impossible," Martin said. "He has to be seeing wrong."

Gene asked, "Are you sure?"

"Not a hundred percent but it looks it," Grabe replied.

"Thank you, Endeavor." Gene turned to Martin. "Is there a private thing that we don't know about?"

"No. I mean, other than Michael Jackson who has that kind of money?" Martin asked. "And it's not like any billionaires are wanting to get into space. He made a mistake. It's another country."

Gene nodded. "Just to be safe..."

"No."

"Yes."

"No."

"Yes, Doctor Kelp is on his way in. He happened to be in Texas."

Martin groaned and stomped his feet. "He's a complete and utter whack job."

"He's the man the air force has on these things."

"Last time I had a run in with Kelp he talked so much I couldn't get away. This whole thing is gonna make me miss my special dinner tonight. The housekeeper is making fajitas. Do you know what fajitas are, Gene?"

"Not really, no."

"They're good but not good if they're cold." Martin placed his hands on his hips and looked up to the board.

"They're in," one of the controllers announced.

Hurriedly, Martin stepped toward the board. "Did they just whiz by?"

"Sorry, I'm late, sorry I'm late," a nervous-sounding voice shouted out. "They finally let me in."

Gene looked at Martin and smiled.

Martin groaned, he knew who it was…Kelp.

Dr. Miles Kelp hurried to the front, excitedly shaking hands with Gene then Martin.

He was a smaller than the average man, maybe standing five foot seven. His identification hung from his neck, dangling just above his skinny fat pot belly. He had what some people would call a skullet: long brownish-gray hair in the back, but the front and top was thin, almost balding. He was excited and energetic.

"Did it come? Did it arrive?" he asked.

Gene replied, "Just broke through the atmosphere."

"Is that it?" Kelp pointed to the blinking dot on the radar screen. It had no numbers, no way to identify it. "Moving that fast?"

"Yes," Gene replied.

"They're crafty buggers," Kelp said. "Above us technologically."

A controller announced, "Confirmed in Texas airspace."

Gene spun around. "Get the Air Force off the ground, find it."

Kelp shook his head. 'I'm surprised they're letting us see them."

Annoyed, Martin spun to him. "Who is them? This is obviously another country, not ours."

Kelp snickered. "Another world you mean. This is an unidentified flying object. A UFO."

"It's not identified, yes," Martin said. "It will be and it won't be from another world."

"They're moving really fast," a controller announced.

Kelp turned to Martin. "Looks like they're heading northwest. Bet they're going for Area 51. I better put them on alert. Maybe a little payback for their buddies."

Martin laughed. "There is no Area 51." He then noticed that everyone looked at him. "Is there?"

"Where do you think I work from?" Kelp asked.

"Doesn't matter." Martin waved out his hand. "It's not another world. Just to be sure we need to alert the president."

"One craft," Kelp said. "It's not an attack. Exploratory mission maybe. But it is…"

"We lost them," said Control. "They just disappeared. Gone as soon as they left Texas airspace."

Martin asked, "Could they have crashed?"

"Possibly."

Gene watched the screen. "Get people out to that last-known location. They had to have gone down. Look for debris."

"Or went invisible," said Kelp.

Martin snapped. "They aren't alien and there is no technology that we know of that makes a craft invisible."

"Alien."

"No. It crashed." Martin tossed out his arm. "And at this rate I am not getting my fajitas."

ARC-373
Day: 4213
Commander's Log Entry 4189

March 11

It has been four long days since we made an emergency landing on Earth. Somewhere outside of Utah, I believe. I can't be sure; our navigational equipment has been damaged.

Does it even matter.

Two days ago, I sent out scouts and they have yet to return.

I will withhold settlement commencement until they bring news.

423 crew and workforce.

4,343 passengers when we left Earth.

The attack and crash-landing has taken 80 of my crew and we lost the lives of 597 passengers. Another hundred are hanging by a thread and 200 have been injured.

Too much to do.

We need to bury our dead.

Commander JV Arlington

FIVE
FEELS LIKE HOME

There was something about it that Nate loved.

When they went to the future, the first time they crossed through the Androski, Nate felt it. The uneasy, washed away feeling of a desolate planet.

It wasn't a world he knew. The Big Blue had changed all that.

When they went to Earth-75, he felt the danger; the world was gray, the sky cold looking, and a chill of doom filled the air.

But this, landing in 1993, was different.

It felt like being home.

The sky was blue, no clouds. It was hot and sunny with desert temperatures.

There was talk as they headed back to Earth, Nate even thought it, what if the Genesis Bandits—as they had been calling them—went back before 1993?

What if 1993 was in full bloom with future technology? No one on the Omni would know because the bandits were jumping at the same time as them.

The spacecraft used the runway which had been designed for TWA passenger planes. It was just long enough.

No one ran toward the runway, nor did they come for the Omni as it taxied to the huge hanger.

Then again, it was invisible.

He could imagine the three workers hearing the high whistle of the engine and feeling the vibration of the ground, not knowing what had happened.

The plan was to put the Omni in the hanger and set up the solar chargers at the rear of the building facing the fence in hopes they wouldn't be seen.

The hanger was old and unused. Cobwebs decorated the high ceilings like party streamers. It was only a minute or two after going into the hanger that the Omni was no longer invisible.

They would stay out of sight in the hanger until it was time to go.

Both Buster and the Omni were dead for the time being.

Tucker disembarked then immediately took an 'I spy' attitude to sneak around the base to find the three workers.

The hanger was at a distance from the rest of Basecamp. Far enough away. Even with the doors wide open, it would be hard for anyone to see what was inside, unless those three workers made regular rounds.

Hopefully, they'd be gone by then.

Nate felt better and left the ship to move about the hanger, enjoying the heat. He took off the flying suit wearing only a tee shirt and thin pajama bottoms. He was amazed at his scar, how fast it was healing.

He felt good for a man who'd died from a hole blasted in his abdomen.

Standing in the doorway of the hanger, he looked out. The small buildings, six of them, were far away.

There was no high technology.

The concrete was covered everywhere with a thin layer of dirt. Nate bent down, grabbing a handful, releasing it slowly through his fingertips.

It felt different. More fine and pure. He couldn't explain it, not even to himself. Maybe it was just all in his head.

"Hey," Rey spoke softly as she approached him. "Drink." She handed him water. "It's hot."

"It's perfect." He took the bottle. "Thank you." He took a sip. "Are Finch and Sam setting up the solar panels?"

"As we speak. The charging countdown begins. What are you doing?"

"Just looking out. I was watching to see if I could see Tucker darting about."

"He said he was stealth and cat-like."

Nate chuckled, then grabbed his belly.

"Still sore?" Rey asked. "Not that you wouldn't be considering you had a hole blasted in you."

"Post surgery I guess."

"I wonder...since they cloned my insides, my stomach and stuff, if you'll have the same issues. We'll have to ask Buster."

"What issues?"

"Too much popcorn always gives me a belly ache. And too much coffee makes me nauseous."

"That's good to know." Nate took a deep breath. "Look at that sky, Rey, when was the last time you saw the sky so blue? So perfect. So uniform."

"The only sky that came close was Earth-150, and that had streaks of pink and purple."

"Do you think...?" He faced her. "Do you think this is the 1993 that Finch was living in or did the Genesis Bandits change things?"

"I don't know. I wonder about that myself. But we won't really know, right? We're not leaving this deserted desert base. The next stop will tell."

"How many more can we do?" Nate asked. "Eventually we have to stop and say this is where we get off."

Rey nodded. "True."

"Where are you hoping to go, Rey?"

"I don't know. Maybe I'll feel it when I get there. Does that make sense?"

"Yep. Because I feel it here. I can be a farmer here in 1993."

"I don't think we'll be here long enough for you to make that decision."

Nate was ready to agree when he perked up at the sight of Tucker walking in the open toward the hanger. "So much for staying out of sight."

In his typical upbeat demeanor, Tucker jogged the remaining way to the pair. "What luck! Can you believe our luck?"

"I'm game," Rey said. "Why are we lucky?"

"They're out to lunch."

Nate choked out a laugh. "I'm sorry, what?"

"There was a sign on the office saying they were out to lunch and would be back at one."

"What time is it?" Nate asked.

"Four," Tucker replied.

"So they're here?" Nate questioned.

"Let me rephrase that," Tucker stated. "The sign on the office said they were out to lunch and would return at one…in 1991. They never came back."

Rey smiled. "That is awesome news. That means we're pretty much safe to charge and go. The nearest town is a mile away. We're good."

"Yep. We slid in under the radar and invisible." Tucker motioned his hand as if it were a plane zooming through the air. "No one will know we're here."

"We think we found them, or close to it."

Kelp's rushed words made Martin stop in his tracks. He was almost free. Almost out the door. He was just about to leave for the day and was happy that his wife told him the housekeeper would stay an extra hour to make sure his fajitas were fresh.

He was happy, excited. The unidentified craft that had made its way into the atmosphere was now the responsibility of the search and recovery team, information that could be relayed to him over the phone.

Martin could be back at NASA in ten minutes if he was needed.

Fajitas were calling him.

Then came Dr. Kelp.

"They found debris?" asked Martin.

"No, they're still searching for that near Texas."

"What do you mean you found them?"

"We think we did, or identified an area," Kelp explained. "I told you them damn aliens were headed to Area 51. Probably trying to free their buddies, who are dead now. Won't they be surprised."

Martin winced. "What are you talking about? I have fajitas waiting."

"Oh, I love those."

"Me, too. That's why I'm headed out."

"Okay you go on, I'll keep you posted."

Martin reached for the door and paused. "Why do you think they went to this Area 51?"

"They didn't make it to Area 51 but they are outside of it and close," Kelp explained. "Radar didn't pick them up, but a maintenance worker heard the craft overhead, soaring by. Then we got a report from Rachel, Nevada. Five people, which is ten percent of the town mind you, called the UFO hotline to report an unseen craft. They heard it loud as if it were close to the ground, felt the vibration, the wind as it passed."

"How was it not seen?"

"AIT, Alien Invisible Technology. I just dispatched a crew to Rachel to interview them."

"So you don't think they crashed?" Martin asked.

"Never did. They turned on their shields as they crossed Texas with a destination in mind. The fact that Rachel, Nevada, heard and felt the craft tells me they were landing. Like a plane coming into a runway."

"Where do you think they landed?" asked Martin.

"I have an idea. There's a base out there, a secret base, but it's been abandoned for a while. It had three workers, but they never came back from lunch one day."

Martin scratched his head. "How did they know about it to land there?"

"They have advanced technology, they probably have stuff that scans the earth. They probably can see those fajitas."

"That's scary. Life from another planet is scary."

"They didn't come to attack."

"Not an attack on our bodies or land."

"What other kind of attack is there?" Kelp asked.

"One that will shake us to the core in more ways than we know. Our beliefs. Seventy-five percent of the world believes we were created by one supreme being. Thinking there's life outside our world is one thing, but knowing it…" Martin said, "is a whole other ballgame."

ARC-373
Day: 4217
Commander's Log Entry 4191

March 15

The scouts have returned.

They made it to a town nearby and reported it wasn't good. Circling the area where we landed, they reported we are in a remote location and should stay here.

We will dig in.

Unload the settlement cargo and begin building a new home.

Commander JV Arlington

SIX

A SHOT IN THE DARK

"When I was sixteen," Finch set into storytelling mode when Nate made a comment about camping. Before that, he'd been content being quiet and sharing one of the logbooks with Rey. "I guess not long from where we are now, my mother, a single mother, decided she wanted to try camping." He closed the logbook.

They didn't have a fire built, instead with the hanger doors closed as much as they could get them shut, they sat inside around a solar warmer. It omitted a blue light and mimicked the sound of a crackling fire.

Finch continued talking to Rey, Nate, and Sam. "We were city people. Camping wasn't on our radar or something we knew how to do. It was the first and last time we went."

Rey asked, "Where did you go?"

"Some chain site, not sure of the name. It was a good two-hour drive," Finch explained. "My mother packed what she could, seriously excited about cooking on an open fire, enjoying the night air. We didn't do a tent, she rented one of the cabins."

"Why did she hate it?" asked Nate. "Or you. Obviously one of you did because you only went once."

"There was no bathroom in the cabin. Shared showers and no internet. My mother didn't know how to build a fire, so she ended up cooking on the stove in the cabin. I liked it. She didn't. My point is, this reminds me of the one and only camping trip I ever took."

Sam chuckled. "Only we cook now in micro-ovens."

The door to the hanger creaked as it opened and Tucker slipped in carrying a box. He set it down to close the door, which still was open a good ten inches.

"Went exploring," Tucker said, lifting the box, then took a seat in the circle. "Anyone wanna know what I found and learned."

"Sure," said Finch.

"Apparently the Three Ms, Mark, Margaret, and Miles, held a three-year contract to live and work here. From what I can gather, their contract expired two months before they just checked out for lunch and didn't come back. So I'm thinking whoever contracted them just didn't know they weren't here. Because everything is still there. Last inspection of this place..." Tucker pulled out a piece of paper. "Was 1985, six years and two contracts before they took off. They stopped checking this place and assumed it was fine. That the Three Ms were still here. Shipments of food and"—he lifted a bottle from the box—"booze kept arriving. Last delivery was two weeks ago. You would think the delivery driver would have known no one picked up the boxes for a couple months."

"Wait." Finch waved his hand. "A couple months...you said the Three Ms have been gone a couple years."

"Obviously someone has been coming back for the goods. Sadly, it's tequila they never took. All the boxes of tequila are shoved in a corner of the office."

"What about food?" Rey asked.

"Nothing that's good now, maybe a can of something called Chef Boyardee," Tucker said. "I think we're safe until we recharge, and we have more tequila than we can use. Where's Buster?"

Sam answered, "He's doing inventory for some strange reason. All charged though. Buster, I mean. With the sunrise at six thirty, the ship will be at full charge by noon, but we can leave by ten with a seventy-five percent charge. Enough to jump, avoid Big Blue, and land."

"I say we do that," Finch stated. "Seventy-five is plenty, we left Earth-75 with much less."

Nate asked, "Will this be the last one? I mean how much longer will the Androski be open for us to go through?"

"Barring we don't die," Sam said, "we can probably jump ten more times over the next month, until it closes."

"The question is," Rey said, "should we? I mean, I'm all for going back to when we left or even when you and Tucker left, but we can't control that."

Finch spoke up, "I think we'll know when we find a place. It'll feel right."

Nate spoke softly, "It feels right now. I would love to stay back here, start a farm, live a simple life. I'll be dead before anything really happens with Big Blue."

"Unfortunately," Sam said, "that's not an option. Now if we'd landed in 1863, yeah, but even in this day and age, you need an ID, social security number. Plus, do we want to chance you changing time?"

"I wouldn't do that," said Nate. "Unless I can make sure it changes the outcome, and unfortunately, that outcome can't be changed."

Rey added, "The Genesis Bandits tried."

"Fuckers," Sam said jokingly.

Shaking his head, Tucker cracked open the bottle. "Shoot. We need glasses. I'll get them."

"No." Finch stood. "I'll get them. I want to grab that other logbook from the ARC and look at that one some more."

"We aren't interrupting your romantic readings with Rey, are we?" Tucker joked. "I mean logbooks are romantic."

"It's the reading them together that's..." Finch stopped then grunted. "Never mind. Who all needs a glass?"

Everyone raised their hands.

Finch smiled. "How many bottles did you get? That one isn't lasting with this crew. That may not be enough."

"Oh, there's more," said Tucker. "You planning on drinking that much?"

"Not me," Finch replied. "I'd like to get in a run in the morning. Never ran in the desert if anyone wants to join me."

"I'm still healing," said Nate.

"Hard pass," said Rey.

"I won't even bother asking you two," Finch said of Sam and Tucker, then stepped back. They were all seated on the ground at the nose of the craft, and as Finch started to board the ship to get the glasses, he paused. His head turned.

"What is it?" Rey asked.

Finch jumped back some then made his way to the door. "Someone is out there, I think." Standing off to the side of the slightly open door, he peeked out.

Tucker joined him. "I just came back, no one is there."

"I'm telling you I saw a light. Small light, a flash, like someone turned on a flashlight."

"Okay, let's watch and look, if they did it once they'll do it again. But it's a clear night, the desert, the sky meets the horizon, still ninety degrees, you may have caught a reflection."

"Maybe," Finch replied, eyes on the outside. He saw nothing again, just a star-filled sky. After a few minutes of extreme focus and nearly holding his breath, he chalked it up to his imagination. After all, they weren't anywhere really. Who would be out there?

SEVEN
EN ROUTE

Kelp was first to board the private plane. There was no entering through the terminal, he had to take a golf style cart across the tarmac. He didn't mind, everyone else had to walk. Kelp felt like a bigshot when he really wasn't. At least it wasn't what he projected to his team.

He was in the first row, aisle seat. Sitting near the window made him somewhat claustrophobic.

It was a government funded flight. An old military craft modernized to look like some sort of commercial airplane, complete with flight attendants, food, and alcohol.

It wasn't a huge plane, two seats on each side of the aisle, about twenty rows.

His front row seat was right behind the kitchen galley. It was an overnight flight of five hours but he was assured a meal was going to be served.

Kelp appreciated that; his team had a long day ahead of them after they landed.

He sipped on a brandy as he watched his team board, each of them nodding an acknowledgement as they passed him. Some of them acted like college students returning from a big game win. They were excited, and rightfully so.

It was a breakthrough, one soon to be released to the public.

Life from another planet had been discovered.

Confirmed, and confirmed on Earth.

They obviously weren't hostile and Kelp wouldn't have his approach be hostile, either.

What did they want? Perhaps they were explorers or maybe they were looking for a planet that could sustain life for their kind. Whatever the case, they were about to meet some of the greatest minds on Earth.

Kelp finished his brandy and held his empty glass up as the stewardess passed him.

"If you don't mind," he said.

"Not at all." She took his glass and went to the galley. She returned with a fresh beverage.

"When will we take off?" he asked.

"I received word we are waiting for one more person," she replied.

"My team is all here."

She gave a look as if to convey that she didn't really have a response, then walked away.

He was one sip into his new brandy when someone walked in front of him to take the window seat.

It wasn't a full flight and for a brief second Kelp wondered why this person was sitting next to him.

Then he saw it was Martin.

"This is a surprise," Kelp said. "You're coming with us?"

"I am. And the itinerary?"

"We'll land at Area 51."

Martin chuckled some. "Up until today I didn't know it existed. Strange considering my role in NASA."

"Well, some clearances don't go to NASA. How did you find out about this?"

"Don't worry about that," Martin replied. "But I will tell you the president is very interested in this."

"Who told him?" Kelp asked.

"He didn't need to be told, he gets to monitor our transmissions with Endeavor. I filled him in on what I know. Which isn't much. He told me that you were given this plane to take a team."

"What else did he tell you?" Kelp asked.

"Not much because he didn't know much. He certainly laughed when I said Area 51."

"Everyone does. He will believe it's fiction. He doesn't have clearance to know more."

"What?" Martin asked in shock. "How does the President of the United States not have clearance?"

"On this, no. Actually, neither do you. I'm not sure how you're here."

"I'm here," Martin said. "What do you mean the president doesn't have clearance?"

"On Area 51," Kelp said. "That is high clearance level."

"Higher than the president?" Martin asked.

"On some issues, yes. But you're here, which surprises me," said Kelp. "You have a full plate."

"I'll make room for this."

"What about Endeavor?"

"It has eight more days before it lands. I heard what Grabe said. I know what you believe. You told me you think they landed and now you have a team."

"Is that what brings you aboard?" asked Kelp.

"When I heard you loaded the plane with some of the best minds, I knew you had something," Martin replied. "Even though you didn't tell me."

"Well it kind of all rolled in at once."

"I see." Martin nodded, then after a pause said, "What rolled in?"

With a change of demeanor and a sip of his brandy, Kelp turned to Martin. "We have a visual. They are exactly where I thought they were."

"Secret Basecamp."

Martin nodded. "Yes. We have a man out there watching. If they leave, we will follow, unless they go back into space. Right now they're making camp in a hanger."

"How many?"

"Looks like three," Kelp replied.

"And they're making camp?" Martin seemed surprised by that.

"Maybe their ship is down. We had a slight visual of it. Very little, though. Of them, we saw them at the door of the hanger."

"Do we know what they look like?" Martin asked.

"Again, my guy was at a distance but he said they appeared humanoid."

"Maybe they're squatters," suggested Martin.

"I'd say that's a good guess. But a ship came in, it went dark, it didn't crash. I think they're camping and repairing their vehicle until they can take off again. We plan on getting them before that. They're a mystery," said Kelp. "I have seen the aliens at Area 51, so has my guy positioned outside of Secret Basecamp. They are not the same."

"So another alien race?" Martin asked.

Kelp shook his head. "My theory? I think they're us."

"What?"

"I always believed most of our UFOs were actually future earthlings."

Martin laughed. "That's absurd."

"More absurd than a reptilian alien life?"

"Future earthlings visiting past Earth," Martin scoffed. "Are they going to look like apes?"

Kelp smiled. "Third movie in the *Planet of the Apes* Series. So, yes, something like that without them or us being apes."

"You think this because they look humanoid?" Martin questioned.

"And the fact that their craft is reportedly similar to the shuttle."

"I think I need one of those drinks." Martin pointed to Kelp's beverage.

"And we'll get you one. And we'll get some answers. Because in about seven hours"—Kelp looked down at his watch—"we're moving in. They won't know what's coming."

ARC-373
Day: 4224
Commander's Log Entry 4198

March 22

The housing units have been constructed and agriculture is beginning to prep what will be our fields.

We lost four more passengers to illness, some seemed rather mild.

We have built a cemetery in a field beyond the housing.

So many have died.

We are still burying them.

Commander JV Arlington

EIGHT
FOUND

Finch couldn't recall the last time he was out of uniform. Other than sleeping, he always looked official. He wore a uniform even under his space suit, but this morning, he felt like himself and felt 'off duty,' so he sported a pair of shorts and a tee shirt. He woke up early, figuring the others wouldn't because they'd been drinking the night before. Although he partook in a little tequila, he didn't drink enough for it to affect him.

It was dawn, only a couple hours before they would take off.

He was in a world that was safe and wanted to enjoy it.

After grabbing some water, he walked through the main hub of the ship and was surprised to see Sam at the computers and Buster seemingly deactivated. Usually when Finch passed him, he'd hear the whirl of Buster's electronics and Buster would say, "Good Morning, Commander Finch, your heartrate is optimal today." Or "Good Morning, Commander Finch, your blood pressure is a few points high, perhaps some beet juice."

But nothing.

"Morning," Finch said to Sam. "Not that I'm complaining, but Buster's still down?"

"I just removed his main box system. Deactivated the bot. He's still running but…" Sam's hand tapped the six-inch square flat object. "He's in here. I am just being precautionary while we're here in 1993."

"You're up early."

"I am. I had a hard time sleeping last night," Sam replied. "After you mentioned that you thought you saw someone, I activated the perimeter sensors."

"And?"

"And it's hard, because we're not in the open. But I didn't see anyone."

"So the lights played tricks on me?" Finch asked.

"My equipment says yes, but my gut says otherwise. However, I can't pick up a person if they're alone. Unlike you because you have a GPS tracker. If they had a vehicle, yeah. But a single person, no."

"So you're watching."

"I'm watching and I'll watch until we take off just to be sure. This is not where we need to be found. Not this early in time."

"I agree. Should I not run?" Finch asked.

"No, go. It's early. Take a radio. Stay clear of the roads."

Finch nodded. "I was going to enjoy running in the desert. It's still cool. And as you said, you can track me."

"Enjoy. I know none of us have gotten to do any of that lately."

"If there's a problem, radio me," Finch told him.

"I will."

"I'll be gone for about an hour. You may want to wake the others. We're at seventy-nine percent charged, better than I'd hoped, so we can take off as soon as we move those charge shields in."

"Take your time. I'll wake them in an hour."

Finch gave a pat to Sam's back. "Thank you."

"Enjoy."

Finch walked toward the door. "We'll be leaving soon."

"Not that I hate it hear, but it's not someplace we can stay."

"I get that. But I want to enjoy a world right now, at least for a run, where nothing dangerous lurks."

"That we know of."

Finch chuckled. "It's 1993, I think we would know if an extinction event was lurking." He gave a nod to Sam and walked out of the ship.

Rey, Nate, and Tucker were sleeping in the hanger and he had to step over them along with empty tequila bottles and bags of snacks. Finch just shook his head with a smile.

They had come from a world where a freak hailstorm or earthquake could happen anywhere or any time.

He was glad they had relaxed. Like them, he was going to enjoy a few more moments and run in 1993 because it wasn't going to be long before they left.

Tucker forgot what tequila did to his body and head. He felt like he had the flu. A horrible headache, stomach churning, and a body that lacked energy.

"Here." Rey handed him a cup of coffee. "Drink."

"Thanks. Trying to get motivated," Tucker said.

"Nate and I have been packing. We're good."

"Where's Sam?"

"On the computer."

"Doing what?" Tucker asked, then waved out his hand. "Never mind. I need Buster and his medical expertise."

"Buster wanted to be powered down until we left 1993," Rey said. "You need to hydrate."

"You seem fine."

"I am."

"Are you an alcohol professional or something?"

Rey laughed. "No, I'm not the Clutch, but I didn't drink that much. Now, he is a professional." She turned her head when Nate approached. "All loaded?"

"All charging equipment is in there. Locked and loaded," Nate replied. "When Finch gets back, we can take off."

"Is he okay?" Rey questioned.

"Yeah, Sam's tracking him. I think we need to clean up out here though. We don't need to leave any remnants of our visit. And..."

"And?" Rey asked.

"Tucker said they had vending machines. I only heard about them, never saw one. I'd like to hit one before we leave," said Nate.

Tucker replied, "That stuff in the machine will be old."

Nate shrugged. "Call it a souvenir. I'd like to take something from it."

"Agreed. We'll put the stuff in a pile by the door." Rey looked around. There were rolled up sleeping bags and a small case with food. She pivoted to the ship's door then raised her voice. "Hey, Sam, we're gonna hit the vending machine and come back to carry the stuff in. Maybe you should radio Finch, give him a heads-up."

"Will do!" Sam replied. "See if the machine has something called Twinkies."

"Okay!" Rey hollered back, then looked at Tucker. "What the hell is a Twinkie?"

Sam could hear it in Finch's voice, the slight out-of-breath sound that he tried to hide.

"How...how far?" Finch asked.

"Hold on." Sam wasn't looking at the computer. He was checking on Buster. "An hour and counting, Buddy," he said to Buster, then rolled his chair back.

"Excuse me?" Finch asked.

"Sorry I was talking to Buster."

"I thought he was down."

"He is. Anyhow..." Sam looked at the computer. "I have you. You're not far. Sending you a beacon through your GPS. Just look at your watch and it will guide you back." Sam clicked a few keys on the keyboard.

"Got it, thank you. I feel dumb."

"You should feel overheated," Sam said. "Temperature is rising out there. But you should be back at a good pace in seventeen minutes."

"Roger that."

"Hey, Finch, how did you get lost? I mean, I know there are no landmarks and even if there were you wouldn't know them. But how did that happen?"

"I picked up some radio station."

"For real?"

"Yeah and this song started playing and I set my pace to the song, then when it was done, I was like wait, where am I?"

Sam laughed. "What was the song?"

"It was a great catchy song."

"What was it?"

"Not sure of the name," Finch replied. "But the words were like, I would walk five hundred miles and I would walk five hundred more."

"That's a song?"

"A good one," Finch said.

"I never heard of it and lucky for you, you didn't walk five hundred miles."

"I'm on the right track now. Thank you. Tell the others I'll be back shortly."

"I will. Right now they're raiding the vending machines for souvenirs." Sam turned his chair and looked at the other monitor. "Looks like they're making their way back."

"Tell them I'll be right back. And Sam, don't mention I got lost."

"I wouldn't do that." Ready to place down his radio, Sam turned his chair and the radio nearly toppled completely from his hands. His screen lit up with motion lights and sensors all moving quickly. "Shit."

"What?"

"Stay put. I mean, stay put. I think we've been found. We have eight, no ten vehicles moving quickly toward us."

"I'm on my way."

"No, seriously, stay put. Fuck."

"Whoa. Language."

"Now's not the time to be Captain America." Sam turned his chair to check where Nate, Tucker, and Rey were. "Come on, come on, come on."

"You said to stay put," said Finch.

"Not you. You stay put. I'm watching the others. Damn it, Finch, they're closing in."

"Who?"

"The vehicles. They'll be here in under a minute. They are definitely headed our way," Sam said. "Stay where you are. This ship and Buster, we can't be found in 1993. I'm out of time. I'm going cloaked."

It was a race against the clock and Sam was certain that Tucker, Rey, and Nate would arrive at the hanger a few seconds before all the vehicles.

He hated to do it, it would eat up the power and delay leaving by another day, but to protect everything Sam worked the controls and went invisible.

"Will you look at this." Tucker walked, palms up with the package in his hand. "Two in one package."

"They aren't glass," Rey said. "They won't break."

"Oh no, they are in their own way a precious commodity," Tucker replied. "I hit the vending machine jackpot."

Nate shook his head. "You ran to the machine and got there first. That's why you got the Twinkies and I got...Doritos. Whatever they are."

"Don't these Twinkies look good, though," Tucker said. "I wish there was another package, I would try these."

Rey laughed. "The sell by date is six months ago. Although my Ho...Ho cakes look interesting."

"Wonder when they stopped making these things," Tucker said.

"Long before us," Nate said. "The vending machine stopped existing when I was a teenager."

"Well, here's to getting back to our time, and this"—Tucker spoke of the Twinkies—"goes into a museum." He stopped walking when he arrived at the hanger ahead of the other two. "Hey, guys, where'd the ship go?"

"Ha, ha, ha," Nate said. "Very funny, I..." He paused. "Where the hell is the ship?"

Before Rey could even ask, the sound of car engines carried to them.

Tucker spun around to see eight black cars speeding their way, followed by two military-looking jeeps. All of them arriving within a second of each other, all of them stopping to a screeching halt seemingly at the same time.

Nate, Tucker, and Rey stood stunned in the doorway of the hanger.

Soldiers, armed with rifles, jumped from the jeep at the same time men in black suits exited the cars.

All of them aimed at Tucker, Nate, and Rey.

"Hands in the air!" one of the men from the cars shouted. "Now!"

"Hey guys," Tucker said softly as he raised his hands, still clutching his package of Twinkies, "I think 1993 found us."

ARC-373
Day: 4234
Commander's Log Entry 4207

April 2

The burying of the dead is complete.
    The fields are ready.
    Morale is up. I have decided to set a holiday in four days.
    We need it.
    I sent four scouts south.

Commander JV Arlington

NINE
Little Green Men

Tucker was a little stunned and knew they had to think fast.

Running and hiding was not an option.

There were weapons locked on them, it seemed everyone had one. The military, men in black suits. The only two without guns were the only ones dressed normally.

Nate spoke softly, "I hope I don't have to hold my arms up too long. This hurts."

"I know," said Rey.

They were a good twenty feet from them. From behind the line of guns, an older military man stepped forward. If Tucker was right, and they used the same insignia in 1993, the man was a colonel.

"Lower your weapon!" the colonel shouted.

Rey replied, "We don't have weapons."

"The tall guy in the middle. Lower the weapon."

"It's not a weapon, it's a Twinkie," Tucker answered. "See." Arms still raised, he turned his hand.

The colonel nodded at a few soldiers and they raced forward.

Tucker thought they were coming for them but they posted on the sides of the door, weapons ready, while the other soldier forcefully flung open the hanger door.

"Empty, sir," said the soldier. "Just a couple of sleeping bags and a small silver case."

"Grab the case, see what's in it, but carefully, it could be a weapon," the colonel said.

Nate sighed heavily. "It's not a weapon. It's camping stuff. Food, flashlights, firestarter."

Tucker spoke through gritted teeth, "Matches."

"Matches," Nate corrected.

Rey shouted out, "We're campers. I know...I know we're trespassing, but is all this necessary?"

The colonel watched as the case was set down at his feet and he nodded for the soldier to open it. They moved back when he did, showing that they were fearful of it being dangerous.

The soldier flipped the lid. "It's weird packaging but looks like food. Not sure what this is." He held up a blue object.

"Put that back, son," the colonel said, then turned again to Tucker. "That's what's in here. How did you know it was empty out here, that no one was around?"

"We knew it because..." Tucker said. "My Aunt Margaret worked here, yeah, she worked here awhile. Nice woman. She went to lunch and didn't come back. Some sort of wage dispute."

A voice spoke up in the back. "Margaret is your aunt?"

"Well, yeah," Tucker answered.

"And she told you about the wage dispute?"

"Um, yeah."

"How is she your aunt?" he said. "Colonel, I think they can lower their arms."

"Oh, thank God," Nate gasped out as he lowered his.

Both the civilian dressed men stepped forward, with the thinner, shorter man leading the way. His hair was longer in the back and he was nearly bald on top.

He stepped close to Tucker, looking at him up and down. "I'm Doctor Kelp. This is Director Martin Weissman of NASA."

"Sweet," said Tucker. "I'm Tucker Freeman."

"Tucker."

"You're looking at me weird, do I look different?"

"No. Just trying to find a family resemblance to Margret. I knew her," Kelp said. "I worked here."

"Here? So you're one of the Three Ms. Are you Miles or Mark?" Tucker asked.

"Miles, and how is Margaret your aunt again?"

"I didn't say." Tucker waved about the Twinkie as he spoke. "She is my mother's sister."

"She didn't have a sister."

"Did I say mother?" Tucker scratched his head. "I mean father. She's my father's sister. Was. She died."

"No she didn't."

"I mean she's dead to us. Big family dispute." Tucker shook his head. "It was crazy."

"Well," Kept said. "She has a brother...in China. Margaret is Chinese."

"Huh." Tucker nodded. "You don't say."

"You don't look Chinese."

"You don't say. I was adopted."

"You are quick. Cut the crap. Where's the spaceship?" Martin stepped forward. "We know you came in a spaceship."

Tucker, Rey, and Nate all laughed.

"Spaceship, like we're little green men?" Tucker joked.

"Spaceship." Martin handed him a rolled-up piece of paper. "We have proof, that photo was taken last night and I believe that's you with the bottle of booze."

Tucker looked at the photo. It wasn't a great shot, a little grainy and green. "Man, the camera does add ten pounds. Is this like paper?"

"It is."

"A picture on paper, that is adorable." Tucker handed it back. "They left. The spaceship people. We were taken captive. Abducted by little green men, but they left. Thank you for the rescue."

Martin's exhale was one of exasperation and in the middle of shaking his head, he looked down at Tucker's pants, then he looked at Rey and Nate. All of them were wearing the white and silver flight suits, with the top part open, sleeves tied around their waist.

"Hold on." Martin reached to Tucker's waist, undid the tied sleeve, and lifted the suit. "JAXA?" He read the emblem. "Captain Tucker Freeman. What the hell is JAXA?"

"Japanese Aerospace Exploration Agency. Formed in 2003."

"It's 1993," Martin said.

"We are well aware."

He reached for Nate's suit. "Are you this JAXA as well?'

"No, I'm NASA." Nate lifted his jacket. "I'm a geologist."

Martin stepped back. "Who are you people? Is there a secret mission we don't know about?"

Rey answered, "Not yet."

"Where are you from?" asked Kelp.

"Might be better to ask when. Me and her"—Nate pointed to Rey—"2043. Him, sixty-eight."

"1968?" Kelp asked.

"2068," Tucker said.

Martin laughed. "You're saying you're from the future? Right." He looked at the colonel.

"Damn Russians," the colonel said. "Take them into custody, we can question them at the other base."

Martin glanced at Kelp. "You don't believe this, do you?"

Kelp shrugged. "But…" He lifted a finger. "If you three are from the future, I guess it's safe to say this Y2K thing didn't happen."

ARC-373
Day: 4239
Commander's Log Entry 4212

April 7

The holiday feast was a great idea. Morale is at its highest I have seen in five years.

The scouts that went south have returned.

They report empty towns that have been abandoned.

They encountered one man, sitting on his porch. He kept repeating the same thing over and over. Delusional, dehydrated.

He was older. They said he looked pale, probably because he was alone and not eating. They couldn't find any food in his home.

They brought him back to the ARC. Dr. Hall is tending to him. Perhaps if we get him well, we can get answers.

Commander JV Arlington

TEN
CAPTURED

Finch was confused about everything. After Sam told him not to move there was no communication until Sam told him, "All clear. Come back."

He didn't say anything about returning quickly and Sam didn't reply to any radio queries Finch made.

What happened? What went wrong? What were those vehicles?

He knew something was wrong, sensed it even stronger as he made it closer, and when Finch arrived back at the Secret Basecamp, he knew.

Sam was outside the back of the hanger. Standing there, waiting, oddly smoking a cigarette.

Finch stopped and exhaled.

Sam looked up and shook his head.

"What happened?"

"They found us," Sam replied. "They came for us with ten vehicles, military and government, as if we were aliens."

"We are. At least to them."

"There were two men with them, one from NASA, one from here, I guess. I picked up what I could listening through Rey's suit. I thought for a second that maybe they would back off.

Tucker tried to convince them they were campers. But they arrested them anyhow. The NASA guy saw the suits."

"Shit."

"Yeah, but on the bright side, the one colonel thinks they're Russian spies."

"So them being from the future is not even an option."

Sam shook his head. "It doesn't seem it. Do you know how hard it was to stay invisible, to not go out there? But I kept thinking, the ship, Buster, the AI we have, cannot be found in 1993."

"They can't."

Sam finished his cigarette and put it out.

"I didn't know you smoked."

"I quit when they hit twenty bucks a pack."

"Really?" Finch asked. "The price came down drastically when Big Blue was spotted."

"Yeah, that's because no one worried about cigarettes killing them. I got this pack from the vending machine. Come on."

"Where are we going?"

"I got a location from the GPS in their suits; I've been tracking them." Sam walked inside the ship with Finch following. He sat down at the computers.

Finch looked at Buster. "He's still down."

"Yeah. For now. Let's see." Sam stared at the screen. "They're still moving. We have a direction. They are moving south toward Vegas."

"Whoa. I forgot Vegas would still be there."

"Yeah, it didn't go down until a year before you left."

"That was horrible. You don't think that's where they're headed, do you?"

"No." Sam shook his head. "They said something about taking them to another base."

"What other base is out there?"

"Let me connect to the satellites." Sam clicked on the keyboard.

"Can you?"

"I'm searching for a connection." Sam leaned back. "I have to connect with one of them, right? Since the internet was not really a thing yet, there's no vast knowledge floating about."

"It's not going to connect," Finch said, watching the 'searching' bar go back and forth.

After a few minutes, it connected, sounding with a tone.

"Bingo. Jackpot," Sam said. "We got a Russian satellite."

"And what?"

"Searching images from the coordinates of this region. If they have a lock on anything, it'll respond. If there's a base in this area, Russia knows about it."

"I keep forgetting about the Cold War."

"Extended a lot longer than we realize," Sam said. "Here we go. The satellite is communicating."

The first image popped up, it was of Las Vegas.

Then within seconds at least two dozen pictures appeared creating a grid of images on the screen.

Some were towns, others were just buildings.

"This is us right here." Sam pointed to the one image. He clicked on it. On the right of the image was intel, including a name. "They coded it WS base. They have it marked as dead."

"What about this?" Finch pointed. "That looks like a base."

"It does." Sam pulled it up. "Huh," he said with a bit of shock and sat back. "It is. About a hundred miles south of here."

"It says Paradise Ranch. US Military Highly Classified."

"It does."

"It looks like a base."

"It is. Look at the code name they gave it." Sam pointed.

"Area 51. That's what we knew it as. Since the forties of last century, I believe."

"It was like alien and UFO shit, right?" Sam asked.

"That was what they said," Finch replied.

"My guess is this is where they're headed," Sam stated. "They know, or at least believe we came from outer space, so it makes sense. If they stop here, we know where they are. Then comes our next problem."

Finch stood upright rubbing his face in thought. "How to get our friends back."

"Yep." Sam nodded. "And to do so before the Androski closes."

ARC-373
Day: 4240
Commander's Log Entry 4213

April 8

The porch man the scouts recovered has passed away. Dr. Hall said he was malnourished and it caused a fever and pneumonia. He remained delusional, never giving his name and often violent.

Commander JV Arlington

ELEVEN
ARRIVAL

After a long ride in the back of a jeep, they finally arrived.

It was hot. The temperature was nearly intolerable but it didn't matter to those who drove them.

Rey sat in the middle between Nate and Tucker, her hands bound behind her back.

They did not speak much.

Rey only hoped that they'd let them go, excusing them as hippie trespassers. But she wasn't sure they were in the right decade for that. Plus, the one man, Martin, noticed the flight suits.

Rey was ready with explanations.

The men who had them didn't seem to believe they were from the future. What bothered her more is they thought they were spies.

They parked inside another hanger where they were led to an elevator and taken below.

After being led from the elevator they were immediately taken into a room, released from their handcuffs, finger-printed, and then left alone.

A few moments after they were brought beverages and fruit. They recognized the oranges and bananas, the other things they did not.

"Anyone know what this is?" Tucker held up a round object.

"That," Nate said, "I believe was called a peach."

"A peach?" Tucker asked. "So this is where the word peach came from. Is it safe?"

Nate nodded. "Very much so. They became rare in the late thirties then they just disappeared. Very big fruit for the southeast."

"Do I just bite it?"

Nate shrugged.

Tucker, after a brief hesitation, took a bite. He chewed slowly then smiled. "This is amazing."

"Why fruit?" Rey asked. "They could have given us anything but why fruit?"

"It's natural," Nate replied. "Unprocessed. That tells me they still think we're aliens."

"We are," said Rey. "Not from another planet but from somewhere that's not here."

"I think," Tucker added, "he means outer space alien. From another planet."

"They definitely don't think we're drifters," Nate stated. "So any attempts to keep the 'we were just camping' rouse is out the window. And went out the window when they saw our suits. So listen, even if they believe we are from the future which you, Tucker, told them, we cannot, I repeat cannot, tell them anything about the future."

"I made the mistake." Tucker slurped his peach. "I won't say a word."

"Good. Apparently, Sam cloaked the Omni," said Nate. "We don't mention them either. I for one will not."

"I for one," Tucker said, "like this peach."

The door to the room opened and Kelp walked in. "I promise to get you more substance as far as food goes. And that you won't be treated like prisoners."

"But we are," said Rey.

"In a way," replied Kelp. "Please sit down."

"Why are we prisoners in a way?" Rey sat down.

"We don't know who you are or anything about you," Kelp said. "Do I think you are Russian spies? No. We have your fingerprints but that may not be helpful. We do know that you were spotted by the Endeavor and you entered Earth's atmosphere at an incredible rate of speed. You also disappeared. We know there was a ship because we have photographs that prove it."

Tucker snickered, then saw the look Kelp gave him. "I'm sorry it's just funny to me that you printed them up on paper. No one does that anymore."

"I'm sorry," Kelp quipped sarcastically. "There wasn't a PhotoHut that could develop them for us in the middle of night."

"What's a PhotoHut?" asked Tucker.

Kelp shook his head. "We also have witnesses...you just shot right over what's called Extraterrestrial Highway. People come here to look for aliens. We're gathering them up now. Trying to keep a lid of silence on this."

Rey chuckled. "Yeah, good luck with that. Pictures and witnesses will be online before you know it."

"I'm sorry?" Kelp asked. "Like radio communications."

"Like the internet," Rey answered.

Nate shook his head. "I don't think the internet is a thing yet. Maybe, but not everyone has it in 1993."

"The internet?" Kelp asked.

Nate held out his hand. "See? He doesn't know."

Tucker decided to explain. "It was around. Internet. Hypertext Transfer Protocol, World Wide Web…"

"Ah, yes," Kelp nodded. "CERN's World Wide Web, introduced it a couple months ago. No worries, it's a fad."

They all softly laughed.

Nate then cleared his throat. "Whatever, it's not a threat of getting out, not in 1993."

"No, hopefully we've contained it," Kelp said. "My coworker fears what this could do to the religious beliefs of the masses if life from another planet exists and God didn't make just us."

"Is that what you think we are?" Nate asked. "Extraterrestrials?"

"I believe you are from another planet," Kelp said. "Yes. My belief is you are from another world. You don't look like ET from the movie, or the alien from *Alien*. My experience is you are humanoid and not little green guys or gray. Those are just fake memos we put out. But humanoid."

Almost with disbelief, Tucker asked, "You have seen aliens?"

"Yes. Yes, I have."

"Where?" Tucker asked.

"Here."

"You have aliens here? Where? Like living here?"

"No, dead." Then Kelp grew nervous. "We didn't kill them, they died when they crashed. Two crashes. Two different times."

Tucker questioned, "And you said they look like us?"

"Can't tell the difference," Kelp replied. "Except, well, they're in a special formaldehyde and are slightly decomposed, missing limbs, so forth."

"I'm sorry," Nate spoke up. "What year were the crashes?"

"They were 1943 and 1968."

Nate looked at Tucker.

"Holy crap. Holy cow," Tucker blurted. "No way. None of this was in the show, man, this is going to be new."

Rey shook her head. "What am I missing?"

"Think about those dates," Tucker told her, then faced Kelp. "Can we see them? Can we see what you have?"

"It's not a pretty sight. We also have stuff from the crash," Kelp said.

Tucker nodded. "We've seen some disturbing stuff, I think it might help if we look."

"Sure, after we're done here I'll take you. We've never had an alive alien before."

Suddenly, Rey gasped and her eyes widened.

Tucker looked at her with a wink. "You get it now, don't you?"

ARC-373
Day: 4244
Commander's Log Entry 4217

April 12

The four scouts that went south have become ill. Dr. Hall has quarantined them out of caution. They have a slight fever, cough, and memory loss.

Too similar to the Porch Man.

Commander JV Arlington

TWELVE
DIAL-UP

A part of Sam felt useless, there was nothing he could do but work on a solution. They had to keep the option of going invisible just in case anyone came back. The monitors were constantly on to track any incoming traffic.

Truth was, they were using a lot of power and it was going to take at least sixteen hours of using barely anything to build up enough power to take off. They couldn't do that until they got their friends back.

"Lunch?" Finch asked as he walked into the room. "I made a pasta meal."

"Uh, yeah, thanks, I'll get some in a minute."

"Are they still there?" Finch sat down next to him.

"Yeah, looks like that's where they're keeping them. So we have to get there and get there fast, take them out...the people holding them, I mean."

"Any ideas how?"

"Fake IDs?" Sam suggested. "Someone that knows a way in, perhaps. Right now, I'm researching data, trying to find anything I can about this place. Maybe even NASA."

"How are you doing that? Do we have access to historical files?"

"Actually, yeah." Sam showed him the computer. "When we were leaving JAXA, I downloaded all the data I could. Stuff that could help us problem-solve the ship if need be. The problem was, they wiped out the data for fifty years. They left everything 1997 to 1991."

"I didn't think JAXA was around then."

"It wasn't," answered Sam. "But they were establishing it for nearly fifteen years before they announced it."

"What about something that may or may not be easier?"

"That's ambiguous. What do you mean?"

"This base," Finch explained. "Everything is still here. Tucker said the deliveries kept coming. The people that contracted this place, obviously a branch of the government, never knew they left." Finch shrugged. "Anyhow, my point is, if they left everything, there's got to be information in those buildings. I'm not sure what kind of computers they had, but they're still there, along with files, and lord knows what else is kept in a secret base."

"If this place is the sister to this Area 51, it makes sense that they never knew they left. This Miles guy who has our friends took them to Area 51. He probably was the one coming for the food, getting the mail, leaving footprints, like downloading data. Making it seem like they were still here."

"So if he kept up the ruse…"

Sam nodded. "Everything is still here. Question is, what was the focus of this secret base?"

"Only one way to find out."

Sam pushed his chair away from the computer and stood. He then stared at Buster, lifting the flat box that was Buster's core.

"You're firing him up?"

"He is the ultimate medical AI. I think he can figure things out if need be, even if he's medical. I can tweak him."

70

Finch sighed out. "Do it. We need all the help we can get."

"You got it." Sam left the room to get the tools he needed.

He wasn't sure what they could accomplish or learn, but exploring the base was one way to find out. Plus, Sam was confident that between him and Buster the technology, if they had any, would be a breeze to get into.

"What the hell is this?" Sam looked at the computer. "For sure this isn't touch screen." He examined the large rectangular box with multitudes of wires all running to a thick white monitor. It was one of four that were set up on an L-shaped table in the room.

Finch, admittedly, hadn't been beyond the reception area, there was no reason for it.

It contained a couch, two chairs, some old magazines that Finch grabbed, and a desk with a typewriter. The power was still on and there was some mail on the desk which Finch took.

Behind the reception area was a door that led down a narrow hallway.

The first door to the right was marked security office. No computer there. Just a desk, corkboard and flag. Across the hall was a small employee breakroom with vending machines.

At the very end of the twenty-foot hall was another door, but they didn't get to that, because they stopped at the room marked 'research.'

Bingo.

At least Finch thought it was.

The moment Sam stepped in, his arms lowered and he belted out his confusion on the computer system. "What the hell?"

"I am sensing a rise in heart rate," said Buster. "Deep breaths will help."

"No, they won't," Sam replied. "I thought things would be higher tech than this."

"Well," Finch said, "for 1993 I think this is high tech. This is kinda similar to what I saw as a kid at the library. But that was probably ten, twelve years after this."

Sam sat down. "I guess this button is the power. They may all be linked and I may have to turn them all on. Buster, do you have anything about 1993?"

"I do," Buster replied. "In 1993, the Milwaukee cryptosporidiosis outbreak was the largest waterborne disease outbreak in the United States. Four hundred thousand people were infected, sixty-nine died."

"Yeah, um, not what I mean. About 1993 technology."

"My apologies," Buster said. "In 1993 Tom Keenan explained how medical imagery could be shared over telephone lines via a computer system."

Finch looked at Sam. "That's closer and helpful. I'm going to look at some of these papers laying around while you dig into that."

"How is that helpful?" Sam's voice squeaked. "Oh my God. I thought I was smart."

"Perhaps I can help you, Sam," said Buster.

Finch just shook his head. He looked at the papers laying around. Some had numbers and coordinates he didn't understand, some notes about meetings. "Oh, look an old twenty-dollar bill."

Sam leaned over, reached out and snatched it from his hand. "I'll take that."

"What for?"

"You never know." He returned to the computer. "What the hell is this?" Sam asked again. "Insert boot disk."

With a whirl of electronics, Buster said, "I believe you are looking for a flat object approximately five inches square that inserts into the slot."

"These poor people." Sam looked around. "Ah, here, it says boot disk." He inserted it into a slot. "There we go. Now it's booting up and booting up…"

"You'll get there." Finch returned to looking around.

"And booting…"

Finch laughed, then he spotted a folder. The label read 'Pioche 1968.' He was about to open it when he heard Sam laugh. "What is it?"

"Look at the graphics. Oh my God. Buster, is there any way you can access data on this?"

Finch watched as Buster looked over the device.

"You're in luck, Sam," said Buster, "like Keenan said about transmitting data, this device is connected to a communication line. If you can find that port, I can access it."

Finch snapped his fingers. "Phone line. Look for a phone line going into the computer, probably in the back, that's how they did it. Using a modem."

Sam rumbled, "So barbaric."

Finch walked over and started to examine the computer. He didn't recall dial-up modems but he remembered his mother joking about them. "There. Here." He pointed. "Buster."

"Thank you, Finch," Buster replied, and from his chest extended a wire.

Sam instructed, "Buster, I tweaked your programming. It should allow you to absorb data that is not medical."

"I am connected. Oh. If I were human, I would describe this feeling as freeing. I feel the information flowing into me."

"Cool." Sam turned in his chair. "Anything useful?"

"I am ingesting data now. Perhaps it would be easier to ask me."

Finch did. "Is there a connection between this base and Area 51?"

"Yes. They share information. I cannot access their information, but they are able to access these computers. Running data."

"We're trying to find a way to get our friends out of Area 51," Finch said. "Is there a security clearance, codes?"

"Area 51 is heavily guarded. The technology for the base is considered beyond the normal technology capacity. It is a technology not shared with the general public. This is odd. Lists and data are kept on something called Lotus 1-2-3. Which I am having a hard time reading at this moment. I am pulling it up on your screen, Sam."

The green words appeared one letter at a time across the screen.

"This is scrambled," said Sam. "It makes no sense. Reverse technology. Then there are symbols and…Pioche."

"Pioche." Finch stepped back and grabbed the folder. "Buster is there anything about Pioche 1968?"

"There is a file buried which is password protected. The Pioche incident 1968."

Finch held up the folder. "That's what this is." He opened it and flicked through the contents.

"What's in there?"

"Images of stuff, bad pictures. I can't tell what it is. The rest is just handwritten notes. Useless." He dropped the folder. "Some names, I'll go through it later."

"Perhaps," Buster said, "more information can be found on the laboratory computer."

Finch looked at Sam then Buster. "There's lab here?"

"A laboratory computer."

Sam stood up. "Let's find that lab."

Behind the door at the other end of the hall was a staircase. It went clear down two flights and there they found the lab. It was evident it was the one place deliberately hidden and had been cleared out before the three Ms left.

There were two rooms separated by wall with a window.

A computer did remain in one of the rooms. It was off and the screen dark, and Sam had to plug it in. But this one didn't ask for a disk to boot up.

"Whoa, now we're higher tech," Sam said. "Still bad graphics, though. Buster, can you tap in."

Buster made his way to the computer and connected himself up. "There is a lot of data. Because of my main programming, medical data is importing."

"Medical data?" Finch asked.

"Autopsy reports. Images. Many images."

"Of an autopsy?" Sam questioned.

"No, just autopsy reports, images of other things. I can display them on the screen; however, I feel the resolution of the old monitor would not suffice in understanding the images. Perhaps if I download them we can bring the data back to the ship's computer system."

"That's a great idea," Sam told him.

"I am designed to be a problem-solver as well. More so human problems and dilemmas."

Finch chuckled. "Yeah, so now you can solve our dilemma on how to get through Area 51 security."

"Thank you, Commander Finch. I will do so. Allow me to download the data and I will make that a priority."

Since the tinkering Sam had done, Buster was a slightly different robot than he'd been twelve hours earlier. Although Finch was not happy with the prospect of having Buster, at that moment, he was glad that the 'problem' of the future was going to help them solve the problem of the past that they now faced.

ARC-373
Day: 4251
Commander's Log Entry 4222

April 19

I believe we know what happened to everyone.

The four scouts have died, and our medical staff cannot keep up with the ill. Over thirty-five percent are presenting with symptoms of this mysterious virus.

I have sent two more scouts out to find answers.

We have commenced separating people and families to try to prevent the spread.

We believe we can contain it.

Hopefully.

Commander JV Arlington

THIRTEEN
TO EACH HIS OWN

Martin waited, he thought patiently, for Kelp to return. In a large meeting room on the base, he paced that first hour, sitting and standing, then went to the mess hall for lunch. He was surprised there was an actual mess hall. It wasn't very big—then again, they only had forty people living and working there.

What did surprise Martin was that they had chicken fajitas. They weren't like the ones his housekeeper made and were served on a hot platter, but they were still good.

Two hours and ten minutes after Kelp said he'd be back, he finally returned.

"I'm so sorry," Kelp apologized as he walked in, closing the door. "The one is a chatter box."

"Margret's *nephew*?"

"That's the one."

"How did it go?" Martin asked.

"We fingerprinted them, talked, they want to see the specimens and artifacts from 1968 and 1943. I did tell them the specimens were killed in the crash and it wasn't a pretty sight. That didn't deter them."

"I'm sorry, the what? Are you implying that the stories about aliens here are true?"

"Yes. I was here in 1968, right here."

"That's preposterous."

Kelp shook his head. "No, it's not. You're NASA. What year did they start the design of the Space Shuttle?"

"Oh, that's easy, design plans started in 1968." Martin's eyes widened. "No."

"Yes. Among other things. The second crash, though deadly, had enough technology way beyond our years to help us along."

"And you shared this?" asked Martin. "With whom?"

"Scientists that are involved with us, but it's not common knowledge that they are working with us, so they work on the science and it comes out incredible and ground breaking."

"Do you really think they're the same aliens?"

Kelp nodded. "Oh without a doubt. They want to see them and I do think it's possibly a good idea. I think they're the same species and they'll recognize the tech we can't."

"They look so similar to us. I mean are we sure?"

"Yes." Kelp handed him a folder. "The inferred photos show their craft in the hanger. We have nine witnesses to their massive craft, including Major Nut Job, and a couple polaroids as well."

"Major Nut Job?"

"Used to work here, quit right after the crash in Pioche. At first I thought it spooked him, then, ten years later, after laying low, him and his buddy opened up the first gift and novelty shop on Extraterrestrial Highway. Very popular because they met aliens personally. No one believes him even though he did see them. He was old then, and he's really old now. He saw the craft fly in," said Kelp.

"But it wasn't there this morning," said Martin. "Where is it?"

"I think they left. Which is frightening."

"What do you mean?"

"What if they see how technologically inferior we are and come back with masses? We don't stand a chance."

"And we both know that is a huge fear when it comes to alien species." Martin exhaled and paced some more. "What now?"

"Right now, we're waiting for General Teaks and Colonel Warren. They'll tell us what is next. Our visitors are in their accommodation having salad and eating it like it's a hundred-dollar steak."

"A…a salad. Like tuna?"

"No, lettuce, tomato, right from the mess hall. They said that lettuce is a delicacy to them."

Martin scoffed. "Come on. And you believe they're aliens? What about this crap that they're from the future?"

"Time travel is not possible."

"How did they get the uniforms?" Martin asked.

"Martin, please, they've been here before. Regular visitors, but now they just got caught."

Martin held up his hands. "Okay, let's say they are aliens. Let's go with we need them to maybe figure out this tech stuff you're talking about."

"And their watches. I want one. They're in pristine condition."

"What's so special about their watches?" Martin asked.

"They're all the same and I think they transmit, communicate. I don't think you realize how much the tech we gathered from the 1968 crash changed things. Without it, mobile phones wouldn't be in the public's hands until at least 2025."

"They're barely in our hands now," said Martin.

"Just wait. In the next five years almost everyone will have one."

Martin shook his head. "I really doubt that. Anyhow, after you get their tech and talk to them, what then? What happens to them?"

"I don't know." Kelp shrugged. "That is out of our hands."

"Is it? I mean, really, is it out of our hands?"

At that moment the door opened and General Teaks along with Colonel Warren, who'd been with them when they apprehended the visitors, walked in.

"Gentlemen." Teaks extended his hand to Martin. "Nice to meet you." He faced Kelp. "How did it go with our visitors?"

"Good. They want to see Dolan Springs and Pioche," said Kelp.

"You think that's a good idea?" asked Teaks.

Kelp nodded. "I do, at least let them look at the tech. It doesn't work, or at least we can't get it to work."

Colonel Warren interjected, "It smashed. Do you think they'll know it?"

"Oh, without a doubt," Kelp replied. "I believe they're from the same planet."

"Good," said General Warren. "Let them eat their salads, the president wants to meet them, and he is looking forward to seeing what we have here as well."

Kelp's eyes widened. "He knows?"

"Oh, yeah, he was pretty excited about it," Teaks said. "Disappointed that the little green man photos we put out were fake."

Martin slightly lifted his hand. "I'm curious, why did you issue fake photos?"

Warren answered, "They did that back in the forties because there were witnesses and people saw things. It was better to put out fakes that people didn't believe than to tell them an alien species looks like us. After all, they could walk among us."

"And may already," added Teaks. "That's why we need to find out what is different about them so we can spot them. Doctor Cyril Wecht will be arriving in two days to get those answers."

"Good God!" Kelp gasped. "He's a pathologist. It's 1993 for goodness' sake, you would think technology has advanced enough to determine that without cutting into them. This isn't 1968."

"Wait," Martin interrupted. "You said they were killed in the crash. Are you saying they survived?"

"It was a different time twenty-five years ago," replied Kelp. "It's a different time now. You can't do this. Keep them, study them."

"We need to know their differences and weaknesses," Teaks stated firmly. "They'll be given a lethal injection beforehand."

Colonel Warren added, "It'll be humane, even though, as we know...they aren't human."

ARC-373
Day: 4260
Commander's Log Entry 4230

April 29

We are losing the battle with the illness.
    No one has improved.
    The only positive is that we have managed to keep fifty percent of our population healthy.
    No new cases in two days.
    That is a good sign.
    The scouts have not returned.

Commander JV Arlington

FOURTEEN
INFO SORTING

"What are we looking at?" Finch stared at the computer screen and at the black-and-white images.

"Bad images from a long time ago," Sam replied. "I mean, these were taken in 1968. A hundred years before my ship left."

"Buster, do you know what these are?" Finch asked.

"From the notes they are pieces of the wreckage. There are classified photos I cannot get into. I will keep trying," Buster said. "From the notes, it also states several pieces of the wreckage were used to advance technology on Earth."

"Makes sense," Finch said. "That right there"—he pointed to an image—"looks like a comm."

"Old cell phone, maybe," Sam suggested.

"Alien technology was pretty similar to what we had in our time, more so your time." He stood up straight after leaning into the screen and reached for the bottle of tequila. He undid the cap and poured a small amount into a glass.

"Little early in the day?"

"Yeah, I'll just pretend I'm The Clutch." Finch raised his glass. "Never thought I'd miss him."

"How do you think he's doing in the Genesis Village future?"

"I'm willing to bet he reinvented bourbon, or will." Finch poured another splash. "Buster, what about those autopsy reports?"

"I am able to pull the autopsy reports. To paraphrase, the beings were dismembered and burned before the autopsy was performed. They died from blunt force trauma and it mentions internal organs not dissimilar to humans. But there is something strange," Buster said. "The previous witness notes mention three beings in the Pioche incident of 1968, but there are only two autopsy reports. I have brought them up on the screen."

Sam looked at the images of the handwritten reports. "Maybe there wasn't enough left of the third body to do an autopsy. They did crash."

"So where is the wreckage?" asked Finch. "Are there no pictures of the wreckage?" He then lifted the folder he'd brought back from the building. "There's nothing in here."

Sam shook his head. "Just the ones from 1943."

"Commander Finch, it appears those are encrypted as well."

"What the hell? Okay, okay..." Finch waved his hand about. "We need to get in there and get our friends and get the hell out."

"Perhaps you could both be delivery drivers," Buster suggested. "It appears that the same truck that drops off items here each Tuesday then goes there."

Sam glanced at Finch. "That's a thought. Hijack them and their uniforms?"

"Hey, Buster..." Finch looked at the folder. "Any information about a Major NJ?" Finch lifted three pink pieces of paper. "Apparently, he called three times months before they left this place about wanting something back at his shop. Someone scribbled Major NJ on the note."

"Let me see." Sam took one of the notes, and read it, "While you were out B, Collins called. Try that name, too. Maybe the Major NJ is code for something. He didn't leave a number."

"There is no Major NJ," Buster replied. "There is coming up a Major William Collins. Former employee. Signed off on wreckage retrieval in 1968, but nothing after. No documents found."

"Oh, well." Finch shrugged. "Not that it matters. I just found it curious."

"But it does," Sam said and stood up. "Maybe someone that used to work there could be the key to getting us in."

"How are we going to find him?"

"I have an idea." Sam hurried out the door of the ship.

Finch followed.

With Buster moving at his robot pace, trailing the field, Finch walked back into the building to see Sam rummaging behind the reception desk.

"What are you doing, Sam?"

"Ha!" He dropped a one-inch-thick book on the desk. The cover read, *White Pages of the Greater Lincoln County Area.*

"What is that?"

"Apparently you didn't go to the Relics of the Twentieth Century Museum."

"I am a relic of the twentieth century."

Sam laughed. "That's funny. No, this is a phone book. A lot smaller than the ones in the museum. Back in the day, everyone received one and everyone's name is listed with their number. I'll start calling Bill Collins." He flipped through pages.

"How many William Collins are there?"

"Three. One address is a PO Box. I'll call that one first. That…" He pointed. "Is a landline."

"I know what a landline is, we still had them when I was younger."

Sam pulled the black phone to him and stopped and lifted the receiver to his ear. "What the fuck?"

"What's wrong? No dial tone?"

"There's a dial tone. Look at this thing. The one in the museum had buttons. This has a round thing."

Finch huffed out. "It's a rotary. Your generation just knows nothing. What's the number?"

Sam showed him.

Finch began to dial.

Sam snickered. "Seems so long and tedious. Are you sure that's going to call?"

"What are you going to ask? If he worked at Area 51?"

"If I have to. Hey, it worked, it's ringing." Sam smiled. His smile then dropped just slightly before returning. "Um, yes, sir, what is your address?" Sam pulled a pencil and scribbled on the edge of the desk calendar. "And is that the official name of the road?" He wrote again. "Okay, got it. And how late are you open? Sweet. No not you. Thanks." Sam hung up. "Found him."

"That fast?"

"Yep. It's him." Sam ripped off the corner of the calendar.

"How can you be so sure?"

"Because he answered the phone, 'Thank you for calling ET Paradise and collectable' and it's located on ET Highway."

"That's our guy. Let's figure out where this place is and go."

"They close at four today, let's see where it is on the map, maybe close enough to walk and get there before they close.

If not, they open at seven tomorrow. But Finch." Sam handed him the address. "It's our guy."

Finch looked down at the paper. "It's our guy," he said. "Hopefully he can help us get in there."

ARC-373
Day: 4320
Commander's Log Entry 4286

June 28

Dr. Hall has declared the pandemic over. It has been twenty days since the last infection. No new cases.
We have lost 2,122 men, women, and children.
The scouts we sent out sixty days ago never returned.
We must move forward.

Commander JV Arlington

FIFTEEN
MEET BILL ONE

"Something is up." Tucker paced back and forth in a room that looked like one of those executive lounges he watched on the *Omni-4* television show. Couches, glass tables, a cheesy looking bar with booze, and no one but him, Nate, and Rey in there.

"What do you mean?" Rey asked, as she poured a drink.

"I mean, they're being really nice to us for thinking we're aliens," Tucker explained. "Our quarters are nice, and they gave us a meal. How about those salads."

"Oh my God," Rey gushed. "The salad was phenomenal."

"That lady just looked at us so weird when we asked for more."

"If she only knew. So good."

Nate groaned. "It's not sitting right with me."

"Is your belly burning?" Rey asked.

"Yeah."

"I told you not to add those peppers to your salad, my stomach always burned."

"I'm not you," Nate defended.

"But you have a copy of my stomach." Rey sipped on her drink. "Wonder if he gave you my uterus. Not that it would do you or I any good. I'll never have a child…"

"Oh, stop." Tucker walked over to the bar. "You can still have children."

"First, even if I found a mate, when? I'm serious? Now? In this time?"

Nate spoke up, "It wouldn't be bad. I mean, it's long enough from the destruction and disasters. I could stay here."

"We might not have a choice," said Tucker. "They may keep us forever."

"Doubtful." Rey set down her glass. "I saw *Escape from the Planet of the Apes*, they're gonna kill us."

"No way. They're so nice," Tucker said.

"Until we scare them somehow," Rey replied. "We just need to not say anything about the friends that *left*"—she emphasized the word to convey she was being sarcastic—"us behind." She poured another drink.

"Keep that up and you'll be like Zera when she drank that grape juice."

Rey laughed. "I love that you know that."

With a grunt, Nate stood. "For all we know, we know nothing. If...if our friends were still here, they couldn't hide for long."

"Please," Tucker scoffed. "One time in season five, I think, The Clutch changed his entire appearance to hide on the alien planet."

"What do you mean changed?" Rey asked.

"He was on the alien planet, slid right in there, hid for a whole year. I think that's when the actor broke his leg and he took a leave of absence."

Nate asked, "Are you saying that if we dress like the nineties, we could fit in?"

"Yeah, but, we're here on this base." Tucker reached for a glass. "We've got to get out of here first."

"Maybe the president will believe us," said Rey. "We'll tell him we're from the future."

"He's going to ask for proof. I mean, some of this tech…" Tucker shook his head. "Give me a day and I could advance them a decade, but should we? No. We can't."

"Speaking of the president," Nate said. "You're military, should you salute him?"

"Heck yeah. It's what we do. Who…was the president, Rey?"

"It was either Clinton or Bush," Rey replied. "I can't recall."

There was a single knock on the door, and General Teaks walked in with the president.

Rey whispered, "Bush."

Tucker saluted. "Sir."

"Please, thank you," the president said and shook Tucker's hand. "I'm Bill Clinton."

Rey winced. "My bad." She downed her second drink and walked around the bar. "Mr. President." She extended her hand to him.

He shook it and then shook Nate's hand. "Now, if you'll indulge me, I'll have one of those. If you would be so kind."

Tucker jumped on that. "What can I get you, sir?"

"What's your favorite?"

"This morning it isn't tequila," Tucker replied. "The bar doesn't have much. Basic."

"Bourbon straight," he told Tucker then turned to the general. "General Teaks, if you'll give us the room, please."

"Sir, they could be dangerous."

"I'll be fine. I don't think they're dangerous at all."

"Yes, sir." The general snapped to attention, pivoted, and left the room, pulling the door closed.

Tucker handed him his beverage. "Thank you. I'm going to assume you are Captain Tucker."

"I am, sir."

He pivoted to Nate. "And you?"

"Nate Gale."

"And what was your position on the flight? Obviously, Captain Tucker flew the ship."

Tucker saw Rey's mouth open and he shook his head. The president didn't need to know more than that.

"I am a geologist," Nate replied.

"And you?" He faced Rey.

"Rey Harper. I am, was, a sixth-grade teacher at Cannon Mac." Rey grinned. "Oh my God, this is historical, and so happy to meet you."

"Really?"

"Yes."

"You said Cannon Mac, where is that?"

"Canonsburg Pennsylvania."

President Clinton sipped his drink and nodded. "I love Pennsylvania."

"Me, too." Rey smiled again, tucking her hair behind her ears and tilting her head.

"We need to talk," said President Clinton. "Maybe afterwards."

Rey giggled.

Nate cleared his throat. "No, you don't to talk and I am telling Finch."

Rey snapped a look his way. "Telling Finch what?"

"That you're flirting with the president."

"What?" Rey laughed. "Why would you threaten that?"

"Okay, alright," Clinton spoke up. "She has a boyfriend, just getting to know her. Let's move on. Rey...We couldn't find anything about you three at all. Colonel Warren is under the belief that you work for Russia and that craft is theirs.

Teaks thinks you're extraterrestrials. I find it curious, though, that you salute, and sound and look pretty local."

Tucker spoke up, "We're not extraterrestrials. We told them once we came from the future and it's pretty hard to explain how that is."

"How far in the future?" Clinton asked.

"That's pretty hard to explain as well," Tucker replied. "But those aliens they have in a lab that died, I don't think they're aliens either."

"Time travelers."

"Accidental," Rey said. "We didn't mean to time travel. Ever see the movie *Escape from the Planet of the Apes*?"

"Love that movie."

"Me, too. We're the apes," Rey said.

"You escaped a dying world?" Clinton asked.

"Pretty much."

"Rey," Tucker quietly scolded. "Maybe you had too much bourbon."

"What kind of event, Rey?" Clinton asked. "No, let's ask the geologist." He faced Nate. "What kind of event?"

"One that would sound outlandish to you," Nate replied.

"I see." Clinton sipped his drink and set it down. "I say let's go see what's in that lab and talk more." He calmly walked to the door.

Tucker at first didn't know what to make of the brief meeting. Clinton was cool and calm, and for a split second he thought maybe the president believed them.

Then he saw him whisper something to the general before they followed them down the hall, keeping a distance.

Nate spoke softly, "What do you think is going on?"

"They think we're either aliens or Russian spies, and I don't know which one is worse," Tucker said.

"If they think we're spies," said Nate as they walked, "why are they taking us to the lab and showing us secret things?"

"I think it's the ultimate test," Tucker replied in a whisper. "If we show any recognition of the stuff, then we're aliens. If we don't, they lean toward spies. And again, I don't know what is worse."

"Dolan Springs, 1943." Kelp stood before a steel door. "Nothing really remains. It exploded on impact." He opened the door.

The first thing that came to Rey's mind was 'wasted space.' It was a big empty room with tables and glass cases.

Tucker stepped inside without hesitation. He peered in the cases; they were filled with blackened and rusted pieces of debris, some no bigger than a finger. It was evident from how everything had been placed in the cases that they were trying to put things together.

"The craft contained what we determined was four beings," Kelp explained. "Burnt beyond recognition. You need to know that in 1943, this entire place was built to protect the bits and pieces of the wreckage. You can look around here, parts of the craft are charred, but the real beauty..." He moved from the door and walked across the hall. "Is 1968."

Tucker had to catch up, listening to Kelp's fading voice. He hurried from the room to follow the others.

Kelp opened the door and it was a room, huge and like the other, but this one had more glass cases.

"How many were on the craft?" Tucker asked.

"We guessed two," Kelp replied. "I was working here at the time when everything was brought in. The occupants died from blunt force trauma." His voice echoed as he walked across the room. "This table here contains artifacts we retrieved from the site. Things we think are broken and haven't a clue what they are. But you can clearly see some parts have alien language markings."

President Clinton began looking about. "A lot of these are well preserved. You couldn't figure them out?"

"We've tried, but the technology is far beyond ours," Kelp answered. "This technology was used in helping the first moon landing and the development of the space shuttle."

Tucker made a beeline for the far end of the room. Something in the case that looked like a pharmacist's cabinet caught his eye.

"That case over there, Captain Tucker," Kelp called out, "contains pieces we couldn't figure out at all."

Five objects were in there, each on a separate shelf.

His heart sank when he saw them.

Nate and Rey came over to him, standing on each side.

"Oh, man," Nate said.

"Right?" Tucker shook his head.

Rey whispered, "That's a lower abdomen repair tool."

"And that"—Nate pointed to the second shelf—"is the lever from the lower bay for solar shields."

"And I know what that is, Sam would recognize it right away. The control module from the propulsion system control. It has his symbol on it."

"Excuse me," Martin called out, "do you recognize those objects?"

In an odd occurrence, Tucker didn't reply because he didn't know what to say.

"That other symbol," Tucker whispered, "is the joint logo from JAXA and ESA. It's not alien, not to us." He turned around to acknowledge Martin. "It's not alien to us."

Ignoring the others in the room, Rey asked Tucker, "Did JAXA have another ship?"

"No. Only one that I knew of, the Lola, and we left that in Earth-175. So what was it doing crashing in 1968?" Tucker turned around again. "I want to see the bodies."

General Teaks spoke up, "It's not that easy. There are preparations, clearances."

Tucker pointed to Kelp. "He made it sound easy. He said, 'Sure, I'll take you to the bodies.'"

"Initially," Teaks said, "we thought it was a good idea. I don't think it is now. Especially with all the bells and red tape."

Tucker nodded. "It all changed with the realization that we know what this stuff is."

Kelp stepped forward. "You know those objects."

Nate answered, "We do. And looking at them, we need to see the bodies. Bad shape or not we need to see them."

"I'm sorry," Teaks said. "It just isn't—"

President Clinton interrupted, "Is there a problem with them seeing the bodies? They're prepared for it."

Finally, Martin spoke up, "It's because they didn't die in the crash, but they don't want you to know that."

Angrily, Teaks spun to the colonel. "Get this man out of here."

"Oh, yeah," Martin said. "Eject the Director of NASA. Smart move, asshole. I will not be ejected from this room and I will not stay silent. They want to see the bodies. Take them now. Mr. President..." He faced him. "If these people have information about the craft or those who landed, we need to know."

"Beings," Teaks corrected. "They aren't human. And if by chance they are, they're Russian spies."

Rey said, "As a history teacher, no country had this technology in 1968."

"Then you're alien," Teaks said. "If you know that technology, you know those objects, you know those who died, and it wasn't around in 1968, what choice do we have to believe you aren't from another planet?"

"Oh my God." Rey tossed up her hands. "Were people really this dumb in 1993? You know a movie will come out in 1998 and it's gonna blow this place out of the water."

"Rey," Tucker grunted out her name.

"*Independence Day.*"

"Rey."

"And the writer probably met you." She pointed to Kelp. "Because you're in it." She then faced Clinton. "I love old movies."

Teaks laughed. "Oh, I forgot the time traveler story. Fine. We'll take you to the bodies."

"And I'm afraid," Clinton said, "you'll have to see them without me. I have to leave. Thank you for sharing this."

"Wait," Nate called out as he walked toward his secret service at the door. "Mr. President, can you help us get out of this facility. Just let us live our lives. We don't mean any harm."

"I can't, it's out of my hands. It's not my decision unless you're Russian spies. Then I step in."

"You're the president," Nate said.

"And I just found out about this place."

Rey smirked. "Just like the movie."

"Good luck," Clinton said, meeting up with his team and then just like that, he left.

"If he's not in charge"—Nate pointed to the door—"who is?"

General Teaks smiled.

ARC-373
Day: 4774
Commander's Log Entry 4599

March 7

Today marks one year since we landed and returned to Earth.

A memorial is scheduled for this afternoon. We are different. Our numbers are smaller, but I believe we are finally healing, growing, moving forward.

A declaration has been made that no one who leaves the ARC base can return.

We don't know what is out there.

We are safe where we are.

Commander JV Arlington

SIXTEEN
MEET BILL TWO

"How funny is that?" Sam asked, walking with Finch.

"Not funny at all."

"Yeah, it actually is."

"No, really it's not." Finch paused to take a drink of water, looking up to the sky.

"You were a third of a mile from this place. Out here jogging and lost."

"Sam."

"Yeah?"

"You've been hanging around Tucker too much," Finch said.

"True."

"Want to know what's really funny?" Finch asked. "How we are wearing clothes left behind at that base. We look dated."

"Nah, we're fine."

They really weren't and Finch knew it.

Sam was smaller than Finch both in height and girth and easily fit into the green, nylon jogging suit, but since it was such a stand out color, Sam opted for the blue security pants and an AC/DC tee shirt. Finch on the other hand didn't have much of a choice, the only thing that fit him was a pair of brown trousers and a short-sleeve, white button-down shirt.

To make matters worse there was a small ink stain on the front pocket.

"I hate leaving the ship exposed like that," said Finch.

"We need to be in complete power, in case we need to take off," Sam replied.

"We have to get our friends."

"Buster is working on that."

Finch groaned. "Yeah, I know. I hate him not being disabled, and running about."

"He's not running about. And we need him to find a solution in case this guy can't help us."

Finch's watch beeped, letting him know they were less than a hundred yards away from their destination. Since they were in the desert, he envisioned a one-stop, one-shop little shack in the middle of nowhere.

However, when he heard the noise, he knew that wasn't the case.

The noise of people talking, laughing, and music being played filled their ears.

The buildings came into view; they were approaching from behind. There were only four or five buildings, but multitudes of campers and tents.

Streamers lined the street with little triangles, and as he and Sam walked onto the main road, Finch could see they were walking into a tourist attraction.

"Wow," Sam said. "ET Highway is popular."

"Back in the day, I remember hearing that Area 51 was at one time a myth. I think it still was in 1993."

"Don't you remember?"

"I was one," Finch said, disgruntled.

"At least it didn't take us long to walk here."

"An hour wasn't bad, I just hate leaving everything there."

"I know, but we'll be back soon…maybe not."

"What do you mean?"

Sam pointed. "There's the shop we need."

Finch felt his stomach sink. The shop was there. It looked like an old town saloon with a big porch. And when Finch saw the line of people outside waiting, he knew getting back to the ship and Buster right away wasn't going to happen.

So they planned to wait.

They waited, listening to people talk about Wild Bill the Alien Hunter as if he were some sort of celebrity. Finch couldn't figure out how that happened since social media wasn't a thing. Yet, people lined up waiting to get into the store.

They wore ET shirts and hats, and snapped pictures of everything around them.

Finch kept his eyes forward, wondering how long they would be out there in that long line and hot sun.

Sam tugged on his shirt. "Hey, since this line is long, can we go there?" He pointed. "Maybe after the line will be shorter."

"No."

"You didn't even look."

Finch did. His eyebrows raised. The outside had a huge green-looking milkshake sign with an alien head on a straw. He spoke the name of the business out loud. "Alien Fizzle Snack Shop? We don't have time for a meal."

"Not a meal, just a snack."

"No," Finch repeated. "Besides how are you going to pay for it?"

"I have money."

"You have money?" Finch asked.

Sam reached into his pocket and pulled out the twenty-dollar bill. "Remember this."

Finch laughed. "It's twenty dollars, there is nothing you'll get for twenty? Maybe a soda."

"Let's go, please."

Finch grunted. "Fine. Five minutes."

"Yes." Excited, Sam hurried across the street to the shop. Finch was right behind Sam when they entered the shop.

The bell dinged when they went through the door. To the left was a long counter, and there was ice cream in the counter display.

A woman stood behind the register. She wore a head piece with two spaceship saucers bouncing back and forth.

Another worker, an older man, was at the far end of the counter engrossed in the small box style television that set on top of the counter.

"This is so great," Sam said. "Oh, candy."

"Make it quick," Finch told him and stayed close to the door.

Sam explored the aisles. "Oh, this is so great. We just don't have this, Finch. Nothing like this."

In a grumpy-sounding way, the man watching the television spoke up. "You boys lose your luggage?"

"Huh?" Finch asked.

"You're dressed like you lost your luggage."

"Um, we actually did."

"Damn shame." The man shook his head. "We have tee shirts."

"I got stuff." Sam showed Finch the cake snacks and candy. "I think I'll get one of those fancy Alien Fizzle drinks."

"You don't have enough money for that," Finch said.

"Bet I do." Sam placed his items on the counter. "Ma'am, can I have one of those Alien Fizzle drinks? Make it the big one."

"Want to add the alien straw?" she asked.

"Please. Thank you." Sam turned his head to the man. "What are you watching? Looks interesting."

Finch groaned. "Sam."

Sam made his way to the man. "Whoa, alien ship conspiracy."

The man nodded. "Geraldo Rivera, he knows what he's talking about. He's coming to interview me tomorrow."

"No, way, that's cool, whose Geraldo?" Sam asked.

"He's joking," Finch said. "Why, sir, are they interviewing you?"

"I saw that alien ship fly in and land yesterday. Saw it myself. But I haven't told anyone but Geraldo. They took the ones who did see it and reported it."

"Who took them?" Finch asked.

"The feds."

"Really," Finch replied. "Wow."

"So, like..." Sam leaned into the counter. "What if they aren't aliens?"

"You mean Russians?" the man asked. "Geraldo is examining every possibility. He leaves no stone unturned."

"Man, I love him," Sam said. "But what if they aren't Russians or aliens but...hear me out...from the future."

"Time travelers?" the man asked.

"Yep."

The man laughed. "You're funny. There is no such thing as time traveling. Aliens yes."

Sam shrugged. "Just a theory."

"Not a very good one."

The woman walked over to Sam and handed him a bag and his Alien drink. "That'll be nine seventy-five."

"What?" Sam said in shock.

"Hey, now," the man replied. "We can't charge any less."

"Everybody else does." Sam handed the woman the twenty. "Keep the change."

"You're tipping us?" she asked.

"Sure." Sam sipped the drink. The alien head of the straw pressed against his lips. "Oh, wow, this is amazing. You deserve the tip." He showed the cup to Finch. "Want some?"

"No. Thank you." He turned his head and looked toward the door. "Let's go, the line is short." He gave a tug to Sam's arm.

"Thanks again," Sam said.

"You have been hanging out with Tucker too much."

"You said that before."

"And I'll say it again." Finch walked out of the store and made his way across the street back to Wild Bill's.

It actually was good timing, the line had shortened and Sam enjoyed his drink...loudly, slurping it up during the wait.

Finally, just as they stepped to the door and some people finally squeezed out, an older man, probably in his eighties, turned the sign to 'Closed.'

"What?" Sam asked. "No. No, we've been waiting."

"No you haven't. You got an Alien Fizzle."

"I was parched."

"Sorry. Closed," he said.

"But we don't want to buy anything," Sam said.

"Then why the hell would I keep it open?" he asked, then looked at Finch. "What are you, the IRS?"

"No." Lifting his hand in almost a surrender, Finch spoke softly. "Listen we need to speak to you."

The old man's eyes went to Finch's hands. "Well, I'll be damned." He stepped out and onto the porch. "You guys were on that ship that came in last night. Saw it myself. Got a few polaroids. But the space nazis came and took them."

Sam asked, "Why would you say that?"

"First, call it a hunch." He sat down in a rocking chair. "Second, no one dresses like that anymore. Neck-ed aliens need clothes. What can I do for you?"

105

"Are you William Collins?" asked Finch. "Major William Collins?"

"Bill, call me Bill." He nodded. "I used to be. Now I'm a business owner who pays my taxes, just in case you are the IRS."

"I'm not the IRS," said Finch. "We need to get into Area 51."

"Everyone needs to get into Area 51. I stopped smuggling three years ago when they threatened to close my shop."

"Smuggling?" Sam asked. "You smuggled people in?"

"I did. No more. So if that's what you want—"

"We need to get in there," Sam cut him off. "We need a way in and out. Do you know?"

"I do."

"Can you help us?"

Bill shook his head. "Nope. I can but I won't. You have to understand. Six people from this town, a tourist, and a shop owner were taken this morning to that base. They'll be released, but they didn't take me. Even though they know I saw the ship. Why? They know I know things." Bill tapped his own temple. "But I can't take a chance of them claiming I'm old and crazy."

"What do you know?" Finch asked.

"Things."

Sam huffed. "You think we came on that ship?"

"I do."

"Well we did."

"Sam," Finch said with warning.

"No Finch. Him of all people will believe us." Sam stepped closer. "Look we landed, we need to get back. But our friends are on the base."

"If you were on that ship," Bill said, "how did they get your friends and not you?"

106

"He was out jogging." Sam pointed at Finch. "And I cloaked the ship."

Bill whistled. "My friend said the next ones that come through would have more technology than the previous ones. He predicted that."

"Can you help us get our friends?" Finch asked. "We just need to get them out and back to the ship."

"And you think it'll be that easy? Even if I helped you get them, you'll never outrun the military. Trust me, I know. Besides." Bill rocked back. "You only got two days."

"Two days?" Sam questioned.

"I heard from my contact in there that Cyril Wecht is already coming."

Finch shook his head confused. "Who is Cyril Wecht?"

"A renowned pathologist. They're gonna do to your friends what they did to the ones in 1968," said Bill. "I was there. I quit and took off. For four years they chased me. Life wasn't easy and I copped them a deal."

"What kind of deal?"

"I gave them tech." He nodded and extended his hand to Finch's watch. "That got them off my ass."

"This?" Finch asked.

"Yeah, but the one I gave them didn't work, so they got nothing out of it that I know of."

"What...what did they do to the ones in 1968?" Sam asked nervously.

"They got three from the ship and put two of them down like wild animals, then took them apart. Like they're gonna do to your friends. They begged for their lives," Bill explained. "I got away with one. That's all I could save. We took off. I had to save him."

"You save one from 1968?" Finch asked.

Bill nodded. "It's a whole long story."

"Where is he now?" Finch questioned.

Bill reached backward and gave a quick 'whap' to the door. "Hey! Drop the moonshine and come out from the back. Come out here."

"We're closed!" the man from inside answered.

"You need to come out."

Finch heard the stomping footsteps, almost like a spoiled child. The door opened with a creak and the man stepped out.

ARC-373
Day: 4971
Commander's Log Entry 4678

September 19

We've been discovered.
    Not by a military force or even people, but by these things.
    This robot-looking army.
    They descended on our housing, attacking our people.
    We managed to get many back into the ARC.
    They surround us, hundreds.
    We're safe for now.

Commander JV Arlington

SEVENTEEN
FRIENDS IN LOW PLACES

It was another level down, three security check points, but finally Tucker, Rey, and Nate arrived at the 'room.' No fancy name or anything official, it was just a room.

As a fan of old movies, Rey was ready for a large tubular vat with a body inside. After all, Kelp said they'd been kept in formaldehyde.

But when she walked in, she saw two coffin-sized cases.

"It's almost like a cold freeze," said Kelp. "A way to keep them preserved."

There was a feeling that swept over Rey as she walked toward the two containers. It reminded her of the day she walked into the funeral home to see her family. Two rooms, both containing coffins. She had lost her entire family and husband in that flash flood.

The feeling of fear, trepidation, heart beating over facing what was in there.

The containers were metal with a glass lid. A green light on the side indicated power.

"We'll clear the frost," said Kelp. "Give it a moment."

Tucker, who was usually upbeat and jovial, was serious. His jaw twitched as he approached the container on the right.

He shook his head.

Nate stepped to him, then Rey joined.

Inside was a man. Steam encompassed him and he looked as if he were frozen in ice. It was clearly visible that an autopsy had been performed. His chest held the sutures, and a line went across his forehead.

"I don't know who this is," said Tucker. "Do you?"

Rey sucked in her bottom lip. "No."

"Who is this?" asked Tucker. "That module was from the Lola."

"Maybe you're mistaken," said Nate.

"No. No, I'm not. It was the Lola." Tucker faced Kelp. "How many were in the ship?"

"There were—"

"Doctor Kelp," Teaks spoke with warning.

Kelp ignored Teaks. "There were three. When we arrived at the ship, there were three. There could have been more."

"Three," Tucker repeated and walked to the next container. He arrived before Rey or Nate and when he looked, he turned fast to Rey.

Nate rushed over. His hand slammed against the container and he stepped back.

"Who?" Rey asked as she inched forward and looked.

It was a woman and her features were clearly recognizable. Despite the attempt to stop the decomposing process, her skin had flaked, and her eyes were sunken, but her identity was without a doubt recognizable.

With a slightly whimper, Rey whispered the name, "Sandra."

So out of character for Tucker, he slammed his fist into the container. "This was inhumane. I just...I can't. I want to go back to our quarters. No wait...to that lounge. I need a drink."

"Captain Tucker, it was 1968."

111

"It was inhumane." Tucker looked at Rey. "You make reference to old movies, to the *Planet of the Apes*, well here we are. A moment when we saw ignorance kill our friend."

"Your friend?" asked Teaks. "You know these specimens?"

"People," Tucker corrected. "They're people. And I'm done here." He stormed to the door. "Take us back now."

"Tucker," Nate spoke with reason back in the lounge. Tucker poured a drink, downed it, and poured another. "I get it. This is killing me. But you have to understand, it was 1968. A spaceship lands. It's ignorance, you said it yourself."

"Are you defending them?"

"No."

Rey tried, "I get what he's saying. But we need to look at something else."

"What is that?" Tucker asked.

"Why? Why was Sandra and whoever else that was, why were they here? Why did they take the Lola and go through the Androski? They had to go not long after we left."

"It was a different time," Nate replied. "Okay, listen to what I am saying. We have speculated that the other half of the Genisis mission took the ship, that they jumped time. Why else were things so advanced technologically when we arrived on Earth-75? Right? We know now they didn't land in 1993? It had to be in 2018 if we go every twenty-five years. But, if they left around the time we did in Earth-175 and went through the Androski, they changed time. Therefore, the earth we left had changed."

Rey shook her head. "I don't understand."

Nate explained, "We left a peaceful, changed geological world in Earth-175, no Risers, no robots, to our knowledge. However, the moment we landed on Earth-75 we realized

112

things had progressed dramatically. So imagine what Earth-175 became after that. The Lola fled. I just have a hard time believing there was only three of them."

"So you're saying," Rey said, "that the earth we left wasn't the earth Sandra and the rest of them lived through, even though it was the same time?"

"Theoretically," Nate replied, "if Earth-75 had killer Risers, how bad was it for Quinn?"

"They didn't reproduce," Tucker snapped.

"They're AI, Tucker, of course they reproduced," Nate said. "They just build more."

The door opened and Kelp and Martin walked in.

Tucker, surprised, turned around and looked at them. "No military?"

Martin shut the door. "Look, I'm on your side. You aren't Russian spies because I know their space technology. I also know that our space shuttle looks like a smaller version of your ship I saw in the pictures. If you're saying you're from the future and those from 1968 also were, then the shuttle design plans make sense."

"I can say," Kelp added, "with certainty and to the best of my knowledge, the 1968 team never told us they were from the future. Then again, I was just a lab aid at that time and knew very little. I was sent over to Secret Basecamp to build and design the base after Pioche."

Nate asked. "You said three. No more?'

"That we know of," Kelp replied. "There could have been more, like there were more of you. But we only saw three and captured three, one of which had help escaping. I think he tried to save all three but was shot in the process. He lived, but was shot."

Tucker slammed his glass. "I'm not a man that gets mad. But I am as mad as a bull in an empty field. What in the world would make you people kill them and take them apart?"

Martin answered, "Fear, that's my guess. And they're scared of you now. No one but a handful of people know you landed, so no one will know if you're gone or dead."

"Well that just sucks," said Tucker. "In our time nothing stays a secret with the internet."

Martin chuckled. "The internet? I thought that would be a fad."

Rey replied, "Hardly. It determined elections, trends, I miss it."

"I want to believe you are from the future," Kelp said. "I want to. But how? Time travel isn't possible. Did the future invent something?"

Rey shook her head. "No, the universe did."

"Please," Martin urged. "Please help us to understand so we can fight for you. I can't go to the news without some sort of proof and going public is the only way to stop this madness. How did you get here from the future?"

"To explain the how," Nate said, "we need to explain the why and it's complex."

Kelp pulled up a bar stool and sat down. "Tell us."

Tucker winced. "I don't know that we can. It will change everything. Haven't the bandits done enough?"

Martin nearly choked out the word. "Bandits?"

As if Nate didn't hear that, he responded to Tucker, "Maybe. What do we have to lose? What was our mission, Rey?"

"To save the human race."

Nate nodded. "So we jump-start it, we still try to save the human race."

"Whoa, there," Kelp said. He shook his head confused. "Save the human race."

"The reason for the time jumping," Nate explained. "See there's this planet out there. It was discovered a hundred years before my time, but thought of as a myth. It has many names, but I think it was called Planet X in this time."

"It's not real," said Martin. "Once a year we have to confirm that to the public."

"Oh, it's real," Nate said. "It's coming. It won't collide with Earth, but it will come into our solar system, interrupt the moon's gravitational pull, and the disasters that will hit as a result are unimaginable. Millions, no, billions die."

"They knew it was coming," added Tucker. "And they started to plan. Countries all over the world started to build ARCs, to save as many people as possible. I developed the agricultural system to sustain life while the ARCs flew to a habitable planet."

Rey then spoke. "What we didn't know, and found out later, was that there were areas of the United States that survived. Had we have known, people could have been relocated there. But that was after we left Earth to check out a habitable planet."

Martin shook his head. "But there is nothing in our solar system. Nothing is closer than hundreds of light years away. How did you get to them?"

Nate explained, "The same way we time traveled. See, one day a NOAA satellite from 1993, NOAA-13, just appeared in our solar system and sent back data. It hasn't launched yet—it will later this year but it will get lost. It came back with images of a planet that was Earth-like. We called it Noah. We discovered, well Androski discovered, a wormhole that opens every twenty-five years for a while then closes. We believed the wormhole was a gateway to another galaxy. After all,

NOAA-13 came through it. So we found the Androski wormhole and decided to reverse course the NOAA satellite, hoping it would take us to this planet. This hope for mankind."

Kelp asked, "Did it?"

"Oh, yeah," Rey answered. "But it was Earth a hundred and seventy-five years from when we left. The wormhole wasn't a transport to another galaxy, it time jumped you in increments of twenty-five years. We left Earth in the Omni in 2043."

"Einstein," said Martin. "He said wormholes could be portals of time."

"And that's where I came in," came Tucker. "I left Earth twenty-five years *after* Rey and Nate when the Androski opened again, in the Lola ship. I landed maybe a day or two after them in the same time. But time is a crap shoot. The wormhole is a crap shot. Two other ships, Genesis One and Two, went through at the same time as me but landed twenty-five years earlier than me. There's no controlling it."

"Other ships went through as well," Rey said. "From other countries. Who knows where they went."

"The crew of the Genesis One," Tucker explained, "had a falling out. They divided and a few from the ship went rogue. Those who went rogue took the ship, who we call the 'bandits.' We think they waited for the Androski to open again and went through when we left. They landed earlier and jump-started events badly. Which, in turn, changed everything for Earth-175."

"Which is why," Nate added, "we believe they took the Lola and went through. Landing here in 1968."

"That module," Tucker said, "came from my ship, the Lola. Everything in the mystery case, came from my ship."

"Except one of the bodies," Rey said. "Sandra. She was on the Omni with me when we launched in 2043."

"I'm sorry," Martin spoke sincerely. "I am. This disaster. Can anything be done?"

"No," Tucker replied. "Humanity will find a way organically to try to survive but it won't stop the disasters."

Martin questioned, "Do you think these bandits you mentioned were trying to stop it or find a way for more people to live?"

"Possibly," Tucker replied. "Maybe with the idea to jump-start techno to fix it, get the ARCs off the ground sooner, or build more. They created a mess and didn't go back far enough."

Kelp mumbled, "What if they did...or tried, to go back further? What if they realized that they hadn't gone back far enough and went through this wormhole again?"

"I'm sure they did," Nate answered. "Again, as my friend keeps saying, it's a crap shoot. The Androski tosses you wherever. It was odd that Tucker and the Lola arrived in the same time as us. They knew when they jumped again they could go anywhere."

"I bet they went to 1943," Kelp said. "Only they weren't so lucky."

Tucker shrugged. "Who knows, there were a lot of ships that went through. Who knows how many are out there and where they went. For all we know the bandits are still hop, skipping, and jumping the time fence."

"I'm fascinated about this Androski," said Martin. "You guys found it? It's visible?"

"Once you find it it's hard not to see it," Tucker said.

"Martin." Kelp turned to him. "You have to release this story. You can leave out the doom and gloom but breaking it is the only way to save these people."

Rey added, "Or get us back up there before it closes."

Martin rubbed his chin and paced. "How? How do we get you back up there and prove your story? Do you have proof of any of this?"

Tucker nodded assuredly. "Yeah, all kinds of stuff including news reports. But not on me. It's all on the ship."

"It's gone," Kelp said.

Tucker just stared, then glanced at Rey and Nate apologetically. "Sorry guys. Telling them may be our only way."

Through gritted teeth, Nate spoke, "Tucker, anything they see will jump the timeline. You really think they'll take us to the ship, see the proof, and then just let us go?"

"I don't know," Tucker replied. "Say, Martin, we take you to the ship. Why can't you just let us take off?"

"I can. We can. But...you have to give me something," Martin said. "If we take this risk. We need something. Something we can build on. Maybe, like Doctor Gale here said, if we start working on saving humanity now, billions won't die."

Tucker whistled. "That's a tall order, when and if I show you things, you're gonna see how tall of an order that is."

"We can try," stated Martin.

"I don't know what to give you," Tucker said. "Before we hand anything over we have to go through the what ifs."

"I understand," Martin said. "I give you my word as a family man and a man whose reputation would be on the line. Anything you give us will only be used to benefit mankind."

"Like a cure for cancer?" Tucker asked.

Kelp excitedly asked, "You have that?"

"No. Just tossing it out there."

"Tucker," Rey spoke softly. "I don't care what we do. Whatever you decide."

Tucker placed his hand on her shoulder. "I think we need to make one more jump, Rey. Call it a hunch, but I think one more jump is getting us close to where we need to be." He exhaled heavily. "I wish we could find that missing person from the Lola."

"For them," Rey said, "it's been twenty-five years."

"I know." Tucker tossed his hands up, lifted his glass, and took a sip. "Who was it?"

Unmistakable.

Upon first sight, there was no doubt in Finch's mind it was him.

Bill smacked that door and in twenty seconds, he stepped out on the porch, griping as he did.

"I told you I'm not a tourist attraction," he said. "I hate when you…" He stopped talking and locked eyes with Finch's.

They both stared at each other.

Both stared in shock. Although Finch supposed it was for different reasons.

He looked the same. Older, of course, twenty-five years older. His blonde hair was now gray, but he still had a headful. He was in great shape; one of those movie stars that never aged like normal people.

Finch didn't know how that was considering how much alcohol the man consumed in his life. The thought that he had given it up was a fleeting one because Bill told him to put down the moonshine.

There he was, shocked.

Then he smiled and stepped forward with enthusiasm.

It had been only a couple weeks since Finch had seen him. But he was embracing Finch like a long-lost friend.

And he was.

A friend he hadn't seen in twenty-five years.

Clutch.

ARC-373
Day: 4973
Commander's Log Entry 4679

September 21

We have managed to take one down. The others are dispersing. But my gut tells me they will return.

Commander JV Arlington

EIGHTEEN
WHERE HAVE YOU BEEN?

Bill and Clutch lived behind the store.

They used a trailer home to create a makeshift addition. But the kitchen was in the back of the shop, and they sat around the kitchen table like family getting together.

Bill locked the front door and shut the blind before joining them. "He knew you'd eventually come."

Clutch tossed out his hand. "No, I didn't. I hoped."

"You look good." Finch reached out and gave a swat to his arm. "Older but good."

"Life's not bad. It was for a while, laying low, not earning my keep. But I built things for Bill and eventually, we started this shop. Finch, the eighties were a blast."

Finch laughed.

"How were you able to live in this time?" Sam asked. "I mean no social security number, no ID."

"You live in the desert." Clutch poured a drink for himself and Sam. "Since you were parched."

"Thanks," Sam said. "Maybe I'll use my alien straw with this."

"Be my guest."

"What happened, Curt?" Finch asked. "I mean, when we left you in Earth-175…"

Bill stopped him. "Earth-175?"

"A hundred and seventy-five years from when we took off." Finch paused to calculate. "Uh, 2218. When we left you were staying, you were content. How did you get here?"

"We had to leave. Some didn't want to. Twelve of us did," Clutch answered. "It was a get out or die."

Sam whispered, "The Risers."

"What?" Clutch looked at him.

"Risers. Killer robots. Eliminating humans," Sam answered. "The first jump we did we ended up in Earth-75, um, 2118. They were everywhere. Wiped out almost all of humanity. Tracked humans by bracelets. Which we didn't have. Those bracelets were the kiss of death. One bonus is we picked up Buster."

"Who is Buster?" Clutch asked.

"Oh," Sam answered nonchalantly. "He's a med bot, he's not dangerous, doesn't use the bracelets to track and kill people."

"They didn't need bracelets to track us," Clutch said, "they found us. For about a week and a half it was all good, then they came over the horizon, hundreds if not thousands of them, shooting at us with these weapons. You said 2118? How did that happen? That's only seventy-five years after we first left."

Finch answered, "We met people. We met survivors. The bots had been around since we left, according to them. They built the ARCs."

"What?"

"Yeah. The best we could figure was that someone went through the Androski at the same time as us, but landed earlier and jump-started technology."

"You found a robot in 2118?" Clutch asked. "Ever think it was you that jump-started this?"

"It crossed my mind," said Finch. "Especially when we picked up Buster. But there were other ships that launched. Genesis was missing. With the way technology had advanced, as described to us by the survivors, we figured the bots came somewhere twenty-five years before we left."

"When we were cloaked," Sam said, "we…"

"Cloaked?" asked Clutch.

"Yeah, we got that tech from Buster. We went invisible," Sam continued. "When we were cloaked I was able to hear what was being said to Rey, Nate, and Tucker. A ship crashed in 1968, that was you."

"We didn't crash, I landed it perfectly," replied Clutch. "They just found us."

"What happened to the others?" Finch asked.

"Nine got away." Clutch snapped his finger. "Ben. Ben survived, and so did Quinn. Although I think he passed last year."

"Sandra?" Finch asked.

Bill answered, "She was one of the ones they got. Most of the nine found Curt here over the years. Military got here, I was working on base when that happened."

"Sandra is gone?" Finch felt it when he saw the look in their eyes. He had worked with her for so long, and to him he had just seen her.

"The ship," Sam said. "What happened to the ship? If you landed, where is it?"

"My guess," Bill answered, "is they couldn't run it, or start it, not with all the fancy controls. They were convinced they were aliens. Last I heard from my contact is they took it apart. I believe it was used for The Columbia Space Shuttle. Although they never were really able to replicate your propulsion system."

"And they never will," added Clutch. "That's something they need to figure out on their own as history dictates. I didn't interfere. Not in a conventional way. We can't. History has to play out. Although I am still waiting on the internet." Clutch stared down to the drink in his hands. "What now, Finch?"

"I have to try to get Rey, Nate, and Tucker."

"They got them. You won't get them," Clutch said. "If security was tough twenty-five years ago, imagine what it's like now."

"That's why we're here," Finch explained. "We're hoping Bill can help us. He knows the base. We just want to get them and go."

"You have to stop eventually," Clutch told him. "You can't jump forever."

Sam smiled softly. "Only for another three weeks. It's like musical chairs, when it stops, that's where we stay." He shifted his eyes to Bill. "Can you help us?"

"I can try. Come up with a plan, Bruce Willis my way in there."

"Who?" Finch asked.

Bill laughed. "I can't do anything until I know for sure they're still on the base and where they are. That's a big base, knowing their exact location will be tough."

"Not really. That…" Finch tapped his watch, "is something we can do."

ARC-373
Day: 4978
Commander's Log Entry 4684

September 26

We brought the downed bot into the ARC. Callum in IT has called them Pinheads because of the chip he has found that looks like a needle. He is working on an offensive if they return. He wants to create a computer virus, a worm that will infect the bots and the others.

Almost like the virus that wiped out half our population.

Commander JV Arlington

NINETEEN
The Meet Up

Martin was well aware it wasn't as simple as just walking the three visitors off the base. After all, Martin was a visitor himself. His every move was being watched.

The three weren't just under lock, key, and security, they were also two hundred feet underground.

The positive side was that no one really knew who they were and what they looked like.

The guard paid little attention to who went in and out of the lounge with them.

Plus, the guards, like every other worker on base, believed they were aliens. They didn't know what they were watching out for.

Kelp pulled it off. With a few changes of clothing, uniforms and hats, along with instructions.

Sizes were an issue. Rey, he believed, was the easiest. She wasn't big. She was average height and build. Plus, there weren't many women working at the base. So, Kelp went down to the mess hall. He requested more salads then slipped into the back, took a dietary coat, put the salads on a push cart, along with a name tag that read Jeanie Wasburg, and left. No one noticed.

He did a hand off of the cart and uniform to Martin for him to drop off to Rey while he went onward for Nate.

He was just as easy.

Nate was the same size as Kelp so he collected a pair of dress trousers, shirt, and lab jacket. He didn't need a name tag, the lab jackets around the base were enough.

Tucker was a bit trickier. He was tall and lanky, and his hair wasn't short. He couldn't pass for military. Security and maintenance were the only two things that Kelp could think of, and since they were only three security men he opted for maintenance. He grabbed him blue overalls, plus one of those maintenance tool bags they all carried. He took a name tag for him as well.

Back at their lounge, Kelp had to admit they all looked good when they changed clothes.

"So here's the plan," Kelp said to them. "Nate, you're going to leave here with Martin. Both of you will walk side by side, talking the whole time about innate stuff. Maybe movies. Whatever you do keep it natural and flowing."

Martin added, "We'll walk to the elevator and go up to main floor, leave past reception, and walk to the administration building. My rental car is parked in that lot. We'll leave there and head to the worker building."

Kelp continued, "Tucker and I will go left, talking about different stuff. Tucker, I will be improvising so go with it."

"Yes sir."

Kelp continued, "Martin will pick Tucker and I up at Exit B and Rey up at Exit C."

"Wait," Rey said. "I'm walking alone?"

"Yes," Kelp replied. "It'll be fine. The dishwasher area is in the back. You'll take the elevator to three, make a right, walk the long hall, and at the end, at the door marked Kitchen

Employees Only, you'll go through it. Behind the sink is the clock to clock out. Swipe your badge and go through that door."

"It's important," Martin added, "that you all act as if you know what you're doing."

"No one will be any the wiser," Kelp said. "Fortunately, we're timing this with General Teaks' daily nap. But we are limited on time. We get back to the hanger, and after you've made it worth us losing our careers, you leave. We hold something tangible and hopefully all will be good."

Martin rubbed his hands together. "It's kind of exciting. Such a caper."

"I still don't know what we can give you," Tucker said. "We're still trying to determine what it could be that won't change things too much or badly."

"I promise." Martin held up his hand. "We will use only what we can in the realms of our current technological state."

"Now," Kelp looked down at his watch, "we leave in a few minutes to time this right with Teaks. To make it look good, we'll need to dump the salads to our empty dishes in the cart."

Rey gasped almost in offense. "You want to throw away salad?"

"Good God, man," Nate quipped. "You can't waste produce."

"Obviously," Tucker added, "they don't know how valuable this is if they can just toss out a suggestion like throwing it out."

"It's salad," Kelp said. "And not a very good one at that."

"Bite your tongue. It's a rarity where we come from," Tucker retorted. "Only the really, really rich can get fresh produce. How about I put them in my tool bag. She can take the empty plates from earlier."

Martin asked, "What are you gonna do with salad in your bag? It will wilt."

"Hey now," Tucker said. "A wilted salad is better than no salad. Plus, we can eat it on the ship."

"Fine," Martin grumbled. "Keep the salad. Are we ready?"

Kelp reached for the door. "You and Nate first."

Martin looked both ways before he walked out, and then with Nate they stepped into the hall.

"Casual pace," Martin told him.

"Do you think it will be easy?"

"I do. As long as we get you there before the general wakes up." Martin pressed the elevator button.

"Doesn't it strike you as odd that the general naps?"

"Could you image how grumpy he'd be if he didn't?"

"You could lose your job," Nate said.

"I'm not worried about it."

The elevator opened and a maintenance worker was in there reading something from a chart.

They stepped inside.

"You on the other hand need to worry." Martin made up the ideal conversation. "You're a Pittsburgh Pirate Fan. Please."

The maintenance guy spoke up, "The pirates are doing pretty good."

Martin pressed the floor he needed. "It won't last. "

"I'll hold out hope," Nate said and exhaled.

The worker didn't bat an eye, he kept reading.

He and Martin rode up three floors and they all stepped off.

The worker went one way and Martin and Nate went the other, in the direction of the administration building.

They didn't need to go through that building, just to Martin's car that was parked in the lot. In fact, they walked straight out and no one stopped them.

He hoped the others had it as easy.

Squeak

Squeak

Squeak

Rey moved at a steady pace down the hall to the service elevator. On that floor, where they were, she knew no one would see her or think anything about her as she pushed that cart. She was safe, but the elevator scared her.

She felt like a criminal. In a sense she was.

She took a deep breath and pressed the button.

Someone in the kitchen was going to notice how old the salad plates were. Even though it hadn't been that long, they were older and the dressing on the plates was dry.

The elevator doors opened and Rey exhaled with relief.

No one was in there.

Following directions, she went to the main floor and once off she headed toward the kitchen.

Squeak

Squeak

She entered through the employees' only door, backside first, and wheeled the cart across the huge kitchen to the dishwashing area.

A man in a white tee shirt smoked a cigarette as he loaded dishes.

Home free.

The door was right there and all she had to do was leave the cart, swipe her card, and head out.

"Hold it!" the gruff man barked

Rey felt her stomach twitch.

"Take the plates off the cart, you know the rules." Finally, he looked at her. "Maybe not. You're new."

"Yes I am."

"These the alien plates?"

"Yes."

"No wonder you don't wanna touch them. I got gloves on. No worries." He put his cigarette in his mouth and talked as he balanced his smoke. "What are they like? The aliens?"

"Scary."

"Tentacles?"

"Four."

"Fangs?"

"Two rows. I...I have to go." Rey pointed to the time clock. "It's been a tough day. I feel like I'm gonna throw up."

"Don't blame you. Tentacles and fangs. Have a good night."

"You too." Rey spun and raced to the door.

Please work. Please work, she repeated in her mind as she lifted the card and swiped it. The door buzzed and Rey was out quickly.

She spotted Martin standing outside the car and she rushed over.

"Everything go okay?" Martin asked.

"Yeah, my heart is racing out of control. But I'm out. Where are Tucker and Kelp?"

"They weren't there but we'll go back. You were fast."

"I hope that's all."

"That's all it is. Now, hopefully Tucker will be out shortly." Martin held the door open for her. "Get in. We'll head to Exit B."

Tucker told Kelp the minute he saw the name on the tag that it didn't sit right.

"Oh, you're fine," Kelp told him.

"No seriously." Tucker kept up the pace. "Do I look like Frido to you? I don't even know what a Frido looks like. Heck, I never heard of the name. Is no one named John? Can't I be a John or Tom?"

"Frido is very common in 1993."

"Really," Tucker said with shock. "How odd. People back here must have worked it out, because no one is called Frido and I have an itching feeling, one look at me and I'm busted."

"We're off the elevator almost home free. Who's going to stop you?"

"Hey," a man's voice hollered. "Hey you. Stop."

"I'm ready to run," Tucker whispered when he stopped. "Try to keep up, old man."

"You." The man caught up.

Tucker turned around. He was ready. "Yes."

The man leaned closer looking at his employee tag. "Frido. I have been calling maintenance and I am glad I caught you. Might you come and see what is wrong with my computer. It seems frozen."

"Computer?" Tucker asked. "Heck, I'm your guy."

"Thank you, Frido."

"Um, Frido." Kelp tapped him. "We really need to go. You're needed at the hanger."

"But…I'm…what's your name?"

"John."

"John, what a nice name. John wants his computer fixed. It'll take a second. Where is it?"

"In here." John opened the office door.

Tucker walked in and stifled a laugh when he saw the computer. "This thing is a beast." He ran his hand over it. "My friend Sam would die if he saw this."

"We do get state of the art," John boasted proudly. "This doesn't need a boot up disk. How about that?"

"Holy cow. That's great." Tucker touched the keys. "Yeah, you're frozen." A few more clicks and the computer went dark.

"What did you do?" John asked.

"I shut it down. Do you mind unplugging it for me?" Tucker set his bag on the chair and opened it, looking for a screwdriver.

"Sure, I..." John looked at the bag. "You must like salad."

"I love salad. Unplug."

"You got it."

Tucker lifted the monitor from the flat box which it sat on and set it aside. He braced his hand on the computer base.

"Unplugged," John announced.

"Thank you."

Again, Kelp tapped him on the alarm. "Frido. Time is ticking."

"Then count the seconds. Actually, time me. Go."

Tucker had worked on relic computers before. His grandfather collected them and challenged Tucker to get them running.

Rubbing his hands together first, Tucker dove in.

He pulled the motherboard and then other things. Giddy like a kid, he switched wires, changed a few things on the motherboard and then put it all back together. He hurriedly screwed the cover back on. "And done. Time."

"What?" Kelp asked.

"How long did it take me?"

"I don't know, I wasn't counting."

"I told you to time me. John, plug it back in."

"Okay but is it fixed?" John asked.

"Yep."

"It's fixed?" asked Kelp.

"I told you." Once he knew it was plugged in, Tucker powered it up. "Wow this thing is slow."

"Ha!"

John laughed. "Good lord, you're a genius! I've never seen it boot up that fast."

"Have fun." Tucker shut his bag. "I'm gonna take my salad home. Ready, Kelp?"

"Um...sure." Kelp looked at the monitor. "Yes, let's go."

Tucker stepped out of John's way and into the hall with Kelp.

"How did you do that?" Kelp asked.

"You guys got things a little backwards. You'll figure it out eventually." He walked with Kelp.

"Frido!"

Tucker turned around, John was leaning out the door.

"I just opened a program!" John said excitedly. "It loaded in less than ten seconds. Brilliant." He gave a thumbs-up.

Tucker lifted his hand in a wave and continued walking. "Is that the door?" Tucker asked then pointed.

"That's it."

"Race ya." Tucker took off running twenty feet and after swiping his card, blasted through excitedly with his hands in the air in victory mode.

"Show off." Kelp walked out and joined him.

"There they are." Tucker pointed to the car. "How are we on time?"

Martin stood outside the driver's door.

"Good," Kelp said. "It'll take us almost an hour to get back to the other base. That's when the clock starts ticking. Teaks will be up. I hope it won't take much to get your engines started. Because it won't be long until he comes after us and he'll do it in full force."

ARC-373
Day: 4990
Commander's Log Entry 4694

October 9

They're back. They have doubled in numbers. Callum has yet
to break into their system. We are on the defensive now.

Commander JV Arlington

TWENTY
CAST AWAY

"Ben, I can't…I can't tell you how glad I am to talk to you," said Finch. He held the receiver of the kitchen phone in his hand.

When Clutch told him he was in contact with Ben, Finch just needed to hear from him.

"I'm glad to hear you're happy."

"I am," Ben replied. "It took a while. I still miss my wife and kids. But right now there are no reminders."

"Something Nate says all the time."

"Do you have to go back?" Ben asked. "Can't Bill and Curt help you find a way to stay? It's not a bad time to live here."

"I'm already living here. I was born last year. And I'd be far too tempted not to go see my mother," Finch told him. "I think we have one or two more jumps in us."

"Where are you hoping you'll go?"

"Honestly? Home. My time or in the vicinity. Even Sam's time."

"To all the disasters."

"We know where to go now."

"Finch," Ben said. "It's not going to be the same world. Something happened. Time changed. Things that didn't exist now do, or will."

"I know."

"Can you hold off forty minutes?" Ben asked. "I'm in To-nopah. I'd like to see you."

"Seeing how our friends are captives. I can wait forty minutes."

"I'm on my way."

It didn't take long for Ben to get there. Bill made some lunch to make the wait seem shorter.

Ben looked good, a little rough, but he was sixty and had been working as a mechanic at his own body shop. Unlike Clutch, he had a social security card, license, and bank account.

Ben lucked out.

He took his great uncle's identity, an uncle who passed away in 1992 and Ben knew for a fact no one ever reported it. He would have been the same age as Ben.

The only reason Ben knew his uncle's personal details was because in 2028, Ben's father was on one of those un-claimed money sites and saw his uncle had unclaimed money.

Ben helped them gather the information, submit it in 2028 and they received the small sum of money. Money, oddly enough, from a bank account closed in 2010.

It crossed Ben's mind a lot that maybe he was already in the past.

Time travel was mind boggling and Ben tried not to think of it.

"When do you head back?" Ben asked.

"Soon," Finch replied. "Did you want to go with us? Go back or see where we land."

Ben shook his head. "No. I'm happy where I am."

"I do." Clutch spoke up. "Can I?"

"Really?" asked Finch.

"Yeah, really. I would like that. No offence, Bill."

"None taken. I always knew you'd go back," Bill replied.

"Question." Ben lifted his hand. "How are you getting them out of Area 51?"

"I have a contact." Bill whistled short and loud. "Hey, Sam, quit fiddling with my computer. I know you want to make it better."

"You need Tucker for that. Almost done," Sam yelled from the other room. "Just..."

Everyone waited.

"Is he okay?" Bill asked.

"Guys, we have a problem, come back here."

Bill grunted. "If he broke my IBM, I'll kick his ass."

Finch made his way back to the office first. Sam sat in front of the computer and lights flashed and moved.

"What kind of game did you put on there?" Bill asked.

"It's not a game. I linked this to the watches using mine." Sam lifted his watch which sat next to the computer. He'd taken it apart. "Those blinking lights are our friends. They're moving fast. In a car or something."

"Where are they headed?" Finch asked.

"Looks like this way."

"The secret base," Clutch said. "They escaped."

"Yeah, that's no man's highway," Bill added. "My escape route when I took Curt. If they're headed to the ship, it won't be long before someone figures that out."

"We have to go," Finch ordered and backed up. "Ben, can you drive?"

"Absolutely."

Sam switched the computer screen back to normal and stepped away.

"Sam, the watch."

Sam looked back at it. "It's no good now. I have another on the ship."

"Should we leave that tech back in 1993?'

"Eh." Sam waved out his hand. "It's Bill, if he hid an alien for twenty-five years he isn't sharing this."

Martin felt like a kid entering a toy store or candy shop. His insides twirled with excitement as they pulled onto the base and close to the hanger.

Was it there? Would it be there?

Tucker opened the hanger door and sure enough, there it was.

It was huge. Twice the size of the space shuttle, taller, wider, and longer.

It barely fit into the hanger.

"Still charging," Tucker said as he led them in. The exit door and stairs were down and Tucker ascended the steps, pausing at the top. "There's room if you want to come."

He was followed by Rey and Nate.

As Tucker crossed the threshold he called out, "Finch. Sam."

Martin was trepid, yet excited. He followed behind Kelp and walked up the stairs.

It was nothing like the shuttle.

They stepped into a small compartment with computers and cabinets. There were two doors to his right, and clearly he could see the cockpit.

"What's back there?" he asked Nate.

"Sick bay on the left. Galley is the door on the right. Below are sleeping quarters and storage. The galley is small."

Tucker returned from the door on the left. "They aren't here." He went immediately to the computer system. "Damn screen. I hate it's not touch screen." He sat down.

"What are you doing?" Kelp asked.

"Looking for them."

"Salads are put away," Rey came from the galley. "Where's Buster?"

Martin questioned, "Who is Buster?"

"Looking now," Tucker stated.

"Ha!" Kelp blurted out excitedly. "Those watches are a tracking system."

"And for communication," Nate said.

"Don't ask for it," added Tucker, as his finger clicked. "Buster is exploring the base. He's on a lower level. What the heck?"

"Would Sam let him do that?" Rey asked.

"Not sure why he did." Tucker looked back at Kelp then Martin. Seeing they were looking at other things, he whispered to Rey, "He's AI, he evolves."

"Get him back here," Rey said.

"First…" Tucker sat back. "Odd. I have tracking on Finch. Not Sam."

"Call Buster," Nate suggested. "See if he knows what's going on?"

"Good idea." Nate pressed the communication button. "Buster, you there? Buster come in."

"Captain Tucker!" Buster said with as much excitement as he could. "It is good to hear your voice. You are no longer captive?"

"No, we are not. We are on the ship. So like, hey buddy, what are you doing out there alone?"

"Tucker, the most amazing information can be gathered using the telecommunication method on the relic computer. I am accessing information all across the world."

"That's cool," Tucker said. "Do you know where Finch and Sam are?'

"The commander and Sam went to find a Major William Collins, believing he would be able to get them onto the base to free you. I, however, am able to shut down security there and divert attention."

Tucker cleared his throat when he noticed Kelp and Martin now listening. "That's good. Um, we don't need that. We're gonna be taking off as soon as they get back. Which should be shortly, it looks like they're on the move. Maybe you want to come back."

"May I finish downloading data?"

"Make it quick."

Nervously, Tucker faced Kelp and Martin.

"That guy." Martin pointed at the console. "He sounds very smart."

"He is. But lacks the common sense that he shouldn't go wondering off."

Martin nodded. "He must be young."

"Very." Tucker stepped away from the console. "I think we need to move the ship from the hanger and get it into ready position to take off."

"Just like that?" Martin asked. "No boosters?"

Nate laughed. "No. We take off like an airplane. And don't ask, we won't share that."

"I'm curious as to what you can share. Tell me," Martin said, "how did you get the ship into the hanger."

"Very carefully," Tucker replied.

"And you plan on getting it out...?"

"Very carefully."

ARC-373
Day: 4994
Commander's Log Entry 4697

October 13

They made it in.

Commander JV Arlington

TWENTY-ONE
RISE, SHINE, GO

Ever since his divorce six years earlier, General Teaks had taken a nap in the afternoons. It was his way of mellowing, taking off the edge, and if he didn't get his nap, he was miserable, even if he didn't need the nap. It helped him to stay awake and work longer hours.

An hour and seven minutes was all his nap would be, then he'd wake, have a little coffee and continue with his day.

No one dared to wake him.

It would have to be a dire emergency.

And since his alarm clock went off, Teaks figured all was fine in the Area 51 world.

He woke, put on his pants, combed his hair, all while his coffee brewed. Teaks didn't rush, there was no reason to. After having some coffee, he grabbed his jacket and made his way down to the lab floor.

Everything seemed normal when he got there. He passed the main room, and didn't see Kelp; he did pass an office where John was being silly and giddy as he looked at some sort of spreadsheet.

After going to Kelp's office, he went to the main lab. "Anyone see Doctor Kelp?"

One of the lab workers turned around. "He was with Director Martin. I think they went to a late lunch."

"The mess hall."

"No, I think out."

"Wait. What? Where? Where would they go for lunch that was even remotely close?" Shaking his head and figuring the worker was wrong, Teaks decided to go to the mess hall. He was bit hungry himself.

He walked by John's office and then stopped, knocked on the frame of the door.

"Oh, afternoon General," John said. "My computer is working swimmingly."

"That's good. Have you seen Doctor Kelp?"

"I did. About an hour ago with Frido."

"Who?"

"The maintenance man who fixed my computer."

"He wasn't with the NASA director?"

"The NASA director is here?"

"Never mind, thank you." He left John with the computer and continued on to the mess hall. They weren't there and no one had seen him.

He then tried to locate Martin, but to no avail.

Something was wrong and his gut told him to go to the wing where the visitors were being held.

The door was unlocked and open and as soon as he went in there, he knew what had happened.

They were gone. Their 'space' outfits were in a pile on the couch. Unless they'd developed the ability to go invisible, their disappearance, along with Kelp and Martin, told him they'd left base.

He sought out Colonel Warren.

"They're gone and they took the visitors," Teaks said.

"Are you sure?"

"I'm positive. And I know where they went."

"Secret base?"

Teaks nodded. "We have to get there and fast. Who knows how far ahead of a jump they have on us. If they're alien, their friends might be coming. If they're spies, which I don't think they are, they're going to slip right into society."

"It's fifty-five miles," said Warren.

"How about a chopper?"

"We can get one." Warren lifted the phone. "It'll take an hour to get here."

"That's too long. A plane?"

"Same thing. By the time they get one ready we can be halfway there."

"Alright. Let's get a squad and caravan," Teaks said. "They don't have a ship, not yet. We get there, we arrest them. We keep them under lock and key, and if I have to watch them myself until Wecht arrives, I will."

"You're still going ahead with the autopsy?"

"They're not human," Teaks said. "What choice is there?"

"That was fascinating," Martin stated. "It rolled like a plane and you just need a runway to take off?"

Tucker nodded. "We do. We'll use every bit of this one, punch through the atmosphere, find the Androski and go through."

"I have a question," Kelp said. "You talked about Planet X coming into Earth's rotation…won't you run into it?"

Rey answered, "We almost did. It was right there. Finch saved us."

"Finch?" Martin asked. "The man you are waiting for?"

"Yes."

"And Sam," Nate added. "Right now, Buster needs to get back here. Tucker…"

"I've called him," Tucker said defeated. "He keeps saying he's getting information. I don't know why." He exhaled heavily. "Alright, I think I need to show you guys the Androski. The next time it appears, technologically you won't be able to go through, so no harm no foul." He moved to the other computer across the room, near the cockpit, and pulled up the image of the sky. "Here. See it?" He pointed to it.

"It's like the movie *Predator*. You can't see it unless you're looking. It's huge." Kelp peered closer.

"Yeah, it is, and I'm not sure what the movie *Predator* is and I'm good with old movies."

"Fascinating."

"Hey Tucker," Rey called. "They'll be here in two minutes."

"Excellent. Once they get here, get settled, fire up for take-off and leave." He faced Martin. "We can't thank you enough."

"The Androski information is invaluable."

"And here's something else." Tucker handed him a folded piece of paper. "In 2003 the Space Shuttle Columbia broke up on reentry killing all seven on board. The cause was determined to be a piece of insulation foam that broke off and hit the left wing during liftoff. The damage allowed for hot atmospheric gases to penetrate through the tiles. I have everything noted here."

"Tucker," Nate softly scolded. "Why would you do that?"

"Because it won't affect history."

Rey tossed up her hands, speaking sarcastically, "Why not just tell them about 911 now."

"Because something bigger and worse could happen."

"Wait?" Martin interrupted. "What's 911?"

Tucker just looked at him. A beeping occurred on the tracking computer. He rushed over. "They're back."

"They've moved to launch position," Finch said upon seeing the Omni. "They really did get out."

"Holy cow." Bill poked his head between Finch and Ben from the back seat. "She's huge."

"It's been so long," said Clutch. "I can't believe I am going back on."

Ben asked, "Are you sure?"

"Positive."

"I understand. I would like to go inside as well, even for a few minutes." Ben slowed down.

"A few minutes is all we have," Finch said. "I think we shouldn't wait to go."

Ben parked not far from the Omni which sat on the runway. They all stepped out.

Finch led the way to the craft; the stairs were down ready. As he ascended he could hear Tucker calling for Buster and he hurried up the steps.

"Finch!" Rey said excitedly. "Where's Sam?"

As soon as she asked that Sam walked in.

"We couldn't track you," she said.

"I used my watch to track you." Sam indicated to his empty wrist. "But I have candy for the trip." He lifted the bag. "They had candy."

"Sweet." Rey smiled.

Finch moved to Tucker. "Where is Buster? I heard you calling him."

"He went by himself to the base." Tucker looked at Sam. "He went by himself. Made that decision."

"Shit."

"Yeah."

148

"He's not supposed to do that," said Finch. "That's not good."

Nate was sitting behind the tracking computer and gushed out, "Holy shit."

Tucker turned around.

"Look who we found," Finch said.

Clutch and Ben entered the ship.

"Oh my God." Rey ran to Ben and hugged him. "Are you coming with us?"

"No, I've made a home here."

"I am," Clutch said.

Rey rushed to him and hugged him. "I am so happy to see you. Wow." She stepped back. "You look good."

"So do you."

"Aw, there it is," snapped Tucker. "The Curey Chemistry. I got chills."

Finch asked, "I'm sorry, the what?"

"Curey Chemistry. The super couple name from the show." Tucker pointed out Martin and Kelp. "These guys put their jobs on the line and helped us escape. Martin here is from NASA. Kelp works at Area 51."

"Pleasure." Martin shook hands with Finch. "It's been exciting. Let's get you guys out of here."

"I couldn't agree more. Sam?" Finch asked. "How are we looking?"

Sam joined Nate. "Do you mind? I have perimeter sensors set."

"Be my guest." Nate stood. "Hey, Ben, you made a life here?"

"I did."

"How hard would it be for me to stay?" Nate asked.

"Nate," Rey gasped. "No."

"Rey, there's nothing for me out there. My family is gone. At least here, I won't have to see any reminders."

"Really?" Rey asked. "The moment social media happens in ten years you're going to be looking for your wife. You can't escape the past even if it is the future."

"Hey, guys," Sam called out. "We have company. Coming fast. Ten vehicles. Six minutes estimate."

"Shit." Finch pointed out. "Anyone that's not going, say your goodbyes now. We have to go. Crew. Prepare. I'll get us ready. Tucker?"

"Be right there."

Tucker walked over to Kelp and took off his watch. "Don't be stupid with this."

Kelp smiled emotionally. "Thank you, and I won't. You have my word that this will stay with me."

"Give it ten years then you can do what you want."

Kelp clutched it. "Thank you."

"Thank you."

Finch hollered from the cockpit, "T-minus four minutes."

Rey spun to Sam. "Buster. Do you see him?"

"I got this." Tucker moved to the coms.

"Tucker, now," said Finch. "We got to go. Secure the doors."

"Sam?" Tucker asked, then raced to help Finch.

"I'll call him." Sam reached for the radio. "Buster, you need to get back. Now. ASAP. We're lifting off."

"I am on my way."

"Engines up," Finch called out.

"One, two and three, now four," Tucker said.

Bill, Martin, and Kelp stood there, knowing it was time to go.

The loud whirling of the engines was deafening in the ship.

Clutch approached Bill. "I have to secure this door. Thank you for all that you did for me, my friend."

Bill shook his hand. "Thank you."

Bill was the first to walk out, followed by Kelp.

Ben made sure he gave a quick goodbye to them and Kelp, and after a small hesitation, walked out of the ship as well.

"Guys, they're here. One minute," Sam said. "Another two minutes they'll be on the grounds then the runway."

"Lock it up, buckle in," Finch yelled.

"Finch," Rey hollered back. "Buster isn't here."

"It's now or never. I see them coming."

Sam's head lowered in defeat as he whispered, "I'm sorry, Buster."

Clutch secured the hatch.

The three of them were on the runway and backed up.

Even at a distance, something told Martin to be as far as he could from the rear engines of the Omni.

He and Kelp backed up, and kept backing up.

The heat was intense, but a part of him was in awe over how superior the technology was.

It made Martin proud.

Without interference from future technology, it was a reality.

Space travel would evolve.

He reflected on the strangers, two of which he never met. He looked over at Wild Bill who stood with a man named Ben.

Ben knew the people on the Omni. Was he the missing kidnapped person from the crash of 1968?

And who was the man that got on the Omni, the older gentleman? He knew them too.

Kelp did mention that they knew of only three people on the 1968 ship. Maybe there were a lot more that they didn't know of.

The Omni picked up speed and headed down the runway. It was as they went, through the loud engines of the ship, that Martin heard it.

A whirling and stomp, electronic sounding but there was the voice crying out.

"Wait. Wait. Do not leave me. Please. Do not leave without me. Wait. Wait."

Martin and Kelp both turned around.

Nearly startled from his footing, Martin watched a robot-type being, arm in the air, running. But he couldn't do so correctly. He was slow and sluggish. His upper body and torso seemed newer, white, and his face was nearly human looking. But his legs were mismatched and clunky, like he got them from another robot.

"Wait," he called out.

It was sad, there was emotion in his voice. Sadness and fear as he chased the ship, as if they would stop.

Like a child left behind. He gave up and his arms dropped.

It had to be Buster, the being they talked to over the radio.

Martin, Kelp, along with Ben and Wild Bill raced to him.

"Buster?" Martin called him.

Buster turned around. "They left me."

"Shit," Ben whispered out. "This is it. This is the moment."

"What moment?" Martin asked.

"The moment that changes time and makes it deadly in the future," Ben replied. "This has to be it. It changes things so much that mankind doesn't stand a chance."

At that second a small, four-by-four hatch opened in Buster's chest.

"Remove my controls, my core. Do so, now, and hide it," said Buster. "This is my core. My brain, the rest is just mechanics. I am just a shell of wires, that is what makes me work. It is the center of my intelligence."

Almost before Buster finished his sentence, Ben reached in and snatched it from him, then closed the compartment.

Instantly, his face lost all of the humanistic qualities and looked more mannequin.

Dr. Kelp reached for it.

"A-Uh!" Ben moved back. "I'll take this. I know why I ran from the future, I know what I saw, I won't let this happen." He slipped it into his back pocket.

Martin looked down to the information he held about the future shuttle disaster, then he felt the ground rumble. He lifted his head and saw the Omni take off. "I think that's a good idea. Without it, this thing even looks different."

"They're coming," said Kelp, pointing to the military vehicles headed their way.

Several of them stopped with a screech, and Teaks jumped out of a jeep, eyes to the sky.

"Damn it, damn it." He stomped like a child. "They left." He stormed to Kelp and Martin. "You helped them leave. You helped them escape. What were you thinking?"

Martin answered, "It was the thing to do."

"I should have you arrested."

Kelp snickered. "For what? A crime that no one knows about. About aliens that just wanted to go home."

"When they come back and attack, it's on you."

"Oh, please," Kelp said smugly. "They'll be back, maybe in another twenty-five years, but the way you drink and smoke, you probably won't be around to see it."

"That's not funny...and what is this?" Teaks' tone changed slightly. "Did they leave this behind?"

"Actually." Ben stepped forward. "That's mine. I built it."

Bill continued for him, "I had him store it here. I knew the base was empty. And when we came out to work on it, damned if we didn't see that ship. I immediately called Miles here." He pointed to Kelp. "I told him to get out here, there's an alien ship."

"That is good work." Teaks pointed to Buster. "Even though it has mismatched parts, we're confiscating it. Somehow, I don't think it's yours."

Ben exhaled. "I want it back when you determine it's mine."

"We'll call Wild Bill," Teaks said. "And you..." He faced Martin. "Go back to NASA, asshole."

Teaks waved his arm around, signaling for two soldiers to get Buster and he kept looking at the sky.

Martin knew he was angry and a part of him understood that. He hated that the visitors left, there was so much more to learn from them. But they had a window of escape and they had to take it. He would always remember that.

It didn't take long for Teaks to snatch Buster and load him up. For an hour, Martin stayed with Kelp, Bill, and the new guy, Ben. They made their way to the hanger, just to check in case something had been left behind.

Of course, Teaks had the hanger checked as well.

Martin didn't want to leave until Teaks was gone. He hated that they had the robot. In the hanger, away from Teaks, he spoke to Ben, trying to get some sort of reassurance that Teaks having Buster wasn't going to backfire.

"Are you sure?" he asked Ben. "That they can't get anything out of the robot."

"If that robot told us it was his heart and soul, then I believe it," Ben said.

"You said you ran from the future?"

154

Ben nodded. "When we first landed, we landed a hundred and seventy-five years in the future. After Finch and the others left to try to hop through the Androski back to our original time, hundreds if not thousands of robots descended on our camp. An army, killing those of us they could. A group of us managed to escape. Two ships. Most of the people from my ship have been living here. I know for a fact that neither ship had a robot."

Bill interjected, "They got that bot in, I think, twenty-one something. So if bots have taken over they arrived somewhere between now and the next fifty years. Is this the one? Who knows."

"I do," Ben said. "The robot talked, it knew what to say and it had artificial intelligence. This is the one."

Kelp finally spoke up, "I can take that gadget and learn it."

"Nope." Ben shook his head. "It stays with me. Dies with me. And hopefully, when they go through the Androski, they will get to a better future. I know they will," Ben said. "Because that future I saw...stops right now with me."

ARC-373
Day: 4999
Commander's Log Entry 4699

October18

I have been unable to write, to do anything, all of our defensive forces are fighting an unbeatable foe. We have now
taken to hiding.

There wasn't time to prepare to store food where we're
hiding.

It seems it's every man and woman for themselves. My
heart breaks for the families that are hiding. I can hear the
glass break, the screams of pain.

What is this? What happened to the world so fast?

Commander JV Arlington

TWENTY-TWO
UNFRIENDLY SKIES

Finch felt as if he were holding his breath the entire time, from the runway until they finally took off. Even when they were breaking through the atmosphere, he still felt focused and when they were amongst the stars, he finally exhaled and sat back.

If there was a no seatbelt sign, he would have taken it off, instead, he announced, "We're safe, we're away from them. I'm gonna take a few and just hang out up here until we go through, if anyone has a problem with that, let me know."

No one said anything.

Tucker got up from the co-pilot seat once they finally made it into orbit. "Do you mind if I go in the back?"

"No, go ahead. I need a breather."

"I get that."

"Join us when you're done," Tucker said. "I'll save the surprise until you come back."

What surprise could Tucker have? Admittedly, Finch was curious. He'd go join the others soon, but for that moment, he needed to think.

Tucker left.

Finch was alone in the cockpit.

It didn't take long for him to hear talking and laughter.

Everyone was finally at ease.

Finch was getting there.

How long had he been sitting there, staring out into the abyss, wondering what the next stop would bring?

Where would they jump next?

Would they end up in 1968? Could they crash like the ship in 1968? Or did they crash? Perhaps the ship was shot down.

It was all guess work.

There was so much he still didn't know from their brief time in 1993.

It was hostile, that was for sure and so was Earth-75, and from what he'd heard, so was Earth-175.

He needed to talk to Clutch, something he hadn't had a chance to do. Clutch had information and answers. He was surprised that Clutch left life in 1993, a world he had lived in for twenty-five years.

He was also surprised that Nate *didn't* leave them.

If they hadn't been caught by the space busters from Area 51, 1993 was an option for a moment. A chance at a life before cell phones and the internet took over.

A chance to see his mother, even at a distance.

Now that chance was gone and they had to go somewhere.

It scared Finch, it really did. He didn't let the others know or see it, but it did. They went ahead, they went back in time. Now, if he was right, they'd go back even further.

1943?

World War Two.

1918

The Spanish flu.

What if they went back even farther? At least it was safer then…no one was watching the skies.

Maybe it would be a good thing to go back to the 1800s or even 1700s and earlier. But there was no controlling it. The Androski opened a door to a time at its choosing.

There was a lack of control and Finch hated that.

He knew several things.

They had two weeks, three tops, at the Androski, then they were done for twenty-five years.

If they landed in a bad place at the next jump, they would have to get out fast.

They'd eventually have to stop. They'd eventually have to stay where they landed. They were a dart being tossed at a time board. The bullseye was the prize time.

What were their chances?

He wasn't a praying sort of guy, but in the silence of his cockpit, watching the wonder and beauty of the infinite stars, Finch said a short prayer.

He prayed for their safety and that they would jump to a good place. A place they felt welcomed and safe. A place where they could finally stop.

"Wait, wait, wait, stop." Rey held out her hands. "I know this."

"Well, you're the only one," said Sam.

"No, I do," said Tucker. "Go on, Rey, name the original crew in the 1968 movie *Planet of the Apes*."

"Not the actors, right?" Rey asked.

"Just the crew on the *Icarus*," Tucker said.

Nate swung a fast look at him. "How the hell do you know that?"

"Uh, yeah, I'm a huge fan. In the opening sequence they traveled a day in a minute, Earth's time."

"It's a hundred years before you left," Sam commented. "Crazy."

"It's a classic. Rey?"

"Okay. Taylor, Landon, Dodge, and the chick that died...the one that was supposed to be the new Eve." She snapped her fingers several times. "Stewart."

Tucker clapped his hands. "Yes. That's it."

"Unbelievable." Clutch stood. "I need another drink. Tell me you guys still have my stash."

"All over the place," Rey said. "I'm the only real Clutch wannabe. Plus, Tucker found a case of tequila."

Clutch placed his hand on her shoulder. "It's really good to see you again."

Tucker smiled and shook his head. "I love the chemistry."

"What the hell?" Rey laughed. "What chemistry?"

"You know," Sam stated. "Why does it have to be Clutch?"

"It's the show, you saw it," Tucker said.

"Yeah, I did, but no offence to Clutch in his senior years..."

Clutch yelled from the back, "None taken."

Sam continued, "Rey doesn't have to choose anyone. This isn't a GetFlex show where every man and woman end up together. Or...*Planet of the Apes* with the new Eve."

"Who knows," Tucker said. "What if we end up going back to like the fifteen hundred and the only men she has to choose from don't bathe or wipe their asses?"

Nate laughed. "She still doesn't need a man. She wasn't chosen to go to repopulate the planet."

"Still," Rey said. "I know it's weird, but if we end up somewhere, like maybe hundreds of years ago, when it's safe, I'd like to have a baby, I'm still in that window..."

"Clutch." Tucker pointed to the back. "He'll help you out."

"You're funny," Rey said. "But no offense to Clutch..."

"None taken," Clutch replied from the back.

"If I were to have a child with anyone on the ship it would be Finch," Rey stated.

"Say what?" Tucker acted and replied dramatically, then turned his head. "Oh, Finch, you might be a dad one day."

Finch, who looked as if he knew he'd walked into the middle of a conversation, nodded once. "That's nice." He then sat down in the circle of chairs next to Rey.

"Are you okay?" Rey asked him.

"Yes. Yeah," Finch replied. "Still reeling in the great escape."

"Found one." Clutch returned from the back holding a bottle.

"Nothing has changed," Finch said and stood up again. "Listen. We are going to have to go through. I am fine with taking a few hours, but that's all. The longer we take to go through, the less time we have to turn it around when we land."

"You mean," Nate said, "if it isn't a time we want."

Finch nodded.

Sam suggested, "We can take an hour. One hour, then we go through."

"I think," Rey spoke up, "we're forgetting one important thing. If we go to the future, we go to a future where we left Buster behind."

"No." Clutch shook his head. "You left Buster behind with Ben. We saw what happened when those things invaded and conquered. If anyone will do what they can to stop it, I believe it's Ben."

Nate asked, "Does this mean we are the time bandits we have been talking about?"

Rey shook her head. "I refuse to believe that. We can't have been the bandits, or how else would we have experienced the changed world before we changed it? It wasn't us. But any change we face now was us."

"Can we all agree on one thing?" Tucker asked. "That 1993 had its perks. We got to meet the president, although our history teacher got the name wrong. Okay, can I share our surprise now?" He moved toward the kitchen and stopped. "Keep in mind this won't be a big thing for Clutch. But it was for me, Rey, and Nate. For Sam and Finch, I hope you are as excited as we were." He slipped into the kitchen.

Finch shook his head. "I highly doubt this will be..." He stopped talking and slowly stood up speaking in awe, "Oh my God, is that a salad?"

"Wait. What?" Sam jumped up. "A salad, like an honest to goodness, no processed lettuce salad."

"Iceberg at its best." He handed one to Sam then Finch. "It even wilted a little. Now do you want"—he reached into his pocket and pulled out packets—"French or Italian?"

"I don't care." Finch blindly reached for a packet. "Anything."

Sam took the other.

"And we have one left to share." Tucker held up the last salad. "What's wrong, Rey?"

"You gave them our salads. Now we only have one to share."

"Rey." Tucker tilted his head. "You had several. And it isn't nice to deprive the future father of your children."

"I need a fork," Finch said and stood again.

"Oh, wait." Tucker again reached into his pocket. "Plastic." He handed one to Finch and one to Sam.

Sam was giddy. "This is so great. Candy and salads. Thank you. Listen to that crunch." He put the fork into the salad. "Oh my god."

Unlike when Rey and Nate ate their salads, one piece at a time, Finch plunged his fork into his getting as much as he could in one go. "This is amazing. Thank you. Thank you. I

162

never thought I'd see real lettuce again. I mean, the stuff we had was sort of real but so processed." He took a bite. "And this dressing, wow. What is it?" He looked at the empty packet. "Kraft. We should have Kraft."

"Look at them enjoying their salads," Tucker said to Rey. "Do you feel guilty?"

"No, they get a full salad. I get a few bites."

Nate leaned in to Rey. "You can have my share."

"Or…" Clutch handed her a small cup with booze. "Drink it off."

Rey took the cup.

"Man," Tucker joked, "I sense a love triangle."

Finch stopped eating. "I feel like this is my last meal. I don't know why. I just have a strange feeling."

"No." Sam shook his head. "Maybe our last bit of lettuce and the one and only time we get this Kraft dressing. But it's not our last. I take it as a sign. The next place we land, we're going to hit the lottery."

"Whatever the case," said Finch. "Let's enjoy this time, and then jump through. Wherever it takes us."

Rey, Clutch, and Nate raised their small cups in a 'cheers' fashion.

Clutch downed his drink. "I'm game for wherever we go," he said. "Nothing can be as bad as the eighties."

"Three minutes to entry," Finch announced. "Life support engaged. Systems check."

Tucker reached up to the console above him. "Systems check. All life support engaged."

Finch wished he had a rearview mirror to look at those in the cockpit behind him. He knew they were all life support engaged, but he wanted to visually see it.

He'd prepared them.

Going through could be like the first time again. They could end up facing the blue planet, having to navigate quickly around its gravitational pull and swing through, or it could be like when they went into 1993 and nothing of the blue planet could be seen.

Mentally, Finch prepared for the blue planet to be there. Unfortunately, as he would soon learn, it was not enough.

It was something he had done several times, jumping through the Androski. The actual passing through was not a surprise. The lights, followed by the loss of power. He knew the second that happened, he had to be ready to power up again.

Fast.

Without thought. Power up and possibly avoid crashing into the Big Blue.

He was ready; his life support allowed for him not to lose consciousness.

"Four seconds," he said to Tucker as they moved through the Androski, floating amongst the lights and darkness.

"Three," Finch said. "Two…" and on one he was ready to engage the engines, facing the Big Blue or not.

A part of Finch felt they were heading toward the Big Blue, and he was right. They were moving ahead.

Only, the Big Blue wasn't right there, sucking them in.

When they emerged from the Androski, he saw it, the huge planet, but it wasn't right in front of them like he was expecting.

It was slightly ahead of them, at a distance. Huge, looking familiar, but not where it was when they originally went through. Not even in the same spot it was in Earth-175.

Barely did he have time to question its position when...slam!

Something hit the ship.

Whatever it was hit them hard causing alarms to blare.

"We have right engine damage," said Tucker.

"Where is it?" Finch asked.

Slam!

Something else hit them.

"Right wing," Tucker reported. "Is that what you mean?"

"No," said Finch. "I know where the damn right engine is, Tucker. Where is it? Where is Earth?!"

As that question slipped from his lips, Finch knew why it wasn't there. Ahead of him, the Big Blue was alone, encircled by thousands of moving rocks, some even hitting the Big Blue, as if to say, 'Take this, you big blue bastard.'

A sickening feeling hit Finch's gut. The pings and slams of space rocks hitting them made their own version of devastating music against the structure of the ship. It sounded muffled as blood rushed to Finch's ears when the realization hit. But they weren't rocks and they hadn't flown into an asteroid belt...they'd flown into a debris field.

"Oh my God," Finch gasped out.

"Where's Earth?" asked Rey. "Where is she?" The panic was evident in her voice.

"It happened," Nate stated. "They said it wouldn't happen."

"How far are we?" asked Clutch.

Slam! Something else hit them.

"We have damage," Tucker stated. "We have to repair it."

"It's gone," said Sam. "Earth is gone. The Blue hit her. It wasn't supposed to. They said it never would."

Finch didn't need to hear Sam say it; he had come to that conclusion. In fact, there was a tension in the ship and it had little to do with the structure of the Omni being compromised.

Home was gone.

"Commander!" Tucker said strongly. "We need to repair now."

"No, we need to go back through now. Right now, before something hits us and we're done."

Another jolt, and another alarm blared.

"Turning the ship now. Hold on."

The lights on his controls blinked along with the alarms.

Through the corner of his eye, he saw Sam take off his helmet and disengage his suit. "Sam! Sit. We're going back through."

"Controls say there's a fire." Sam jumped from the seat. "It'll wipe us out before we do."

"Son of a bitch," Finch cursed.

"Just go for it," Tucker told him.

"Give me sixty seconds?"

What was he doing? Why was Sam going alone? Rey undid her belt and followed him. It was hard to move, the gravity was sluggish and she felt like she was running in water.

"Stay back," Sam said as he used the extinguisher to put out the flames in the small area by the kitchen. "We don't need you going up. Your oxygen is still on."

There was smoke everywhere and the flames looked odd, blue and green, as if they weren't real.

Another slam and the ship tilted. Sam blasted the extinguisher a couple more times. "It's out."

Rey held on as the Omni jolted and picked up speed. It was slammed by another object then the power went down.

She didn't know if they lost power due to damage or if they'd gone back through the Androski. But no power meant no life support, and in second Sam was out like a light.

His body went forward, his head hit hard against the counter and then he floated upward. The blood from his wound floated around. Like bubbles of red mercury in water.

Rey moved for him, trying to grab hold of Sam. There were flashes of light through the windows and she knew they'd turned and gone back through. Just as she grabbed his waist, the power came back on and he fell to the floor, thankfully without hitting his head again. The blood splashed around him.

"We're through," Finch spoke into her earpiece.

"We need help," Rey said through the radio in her helmet. "Sam's down."

Rey took off her own helmet, slipping on the blood that had splashed on the floor. She took off her gloves and felt for a pulse. "Come on, Sam. Come on."

He was alive and she exhaled in relief.

Looking around she couldn't reach anything from her position, so she used her glove to cover the bleeding as she yelled out for help again.

Nate was the first one back, then Clutch came a second later.

"He's hurt," Rey said. "This looks bad."

"I'll go to med bay," Clutch responded, stepping over Sam to get to the back.

Nate immediately grabbed for a towel to replace her glove. "He's breathing."

"I know."

"I'm not a medical doctor, but I think he'll be okay. Hopefully."

"Hopefully?"

Nate shrugged. "It's hard to tell, the head bleeds pretty good."

Rey saw Sam's eyes moving. "I think he's coming to. I was afraid, you know, that we just took one too many hits and the ship was dead."

"She's damaged. But we made it through," Nate told her. "We are in the past at some point. We just need to determine where or rather when we are, but that's hard. No Big Blue. Just a speck in the distance."

"What does it matter?" Rey said sadly. "It hits Earth. It destroys Earth."

"We don't know how far in the future that is," Nate said, trying to lift Sam to a better position. "We need to get close to see Earth."

Sam groaned. "What happened?"

"You hit your head," Nate told him. "You got a hell of a gash."

"At least you didn't feel it," Rey told him. "You were out when it happened. We went through the Androski again."

"That sucks for power." Sam stumbled to a stand but gave up and sat back down. "Twice in a row, that sucks a lot out of us. We can't orbit very long."

"Well, we need to take care of your head," Rey told him.

Clutch returned. He stepped over Sam again with the medical bag. "Bandages, glue, stuff to clean him up. Let me handle this. I worked as a volunteer paramedic for twelve years."

"Really?" Rey asked.

"Have to do something, right?" Clutch said.

"Always saving lives," Rey told him, then she looked back when she heard the long, drawn-out 'aw' that came from Tucker.

Tucker stood there. "Sam is okay and you two are just…" He snapped his finger. "Clicking. Curey."

Rey sighed and shook her head.

"Look, Finch needs everyone up front. Time for a crew meeting," Tucker announced.

Rey noticed the seriousness that suddenly took over Tucker. "How bad is it?"

"Let's just say, where or whenever we are, we just had our last jump."

"Nah," Sam spoke up groggily. "We can always repair. We just might have to wait twenty-five years to jump again."

"Take a front row seat." Finch patted the seat next to Tucker's chair. "Tucker won't mind."

"Not at all," Tucker said, walking in with Rey.

Rey sat down. Her eyes focused on Earth. It was there. It looked normal. Then again, when they went to Earth-175 and Earth-75 it looked normal, too. "Whoa."

"Yeah, I know. There she is."

"I can't believe Earth gets destroyed in the future. I just can't. Can you image the destruction that happened before Big Blue slammed into her," Rey spoke softly.

Nate explained as he entered the cockpit, "The destruction would have been nonsurvivable before it even hit Earth. No one would remain. The disasters it caused when it was five hundred thousand miles away were horrendous. When it settled into an orbit at a hundred and eighty it changed the face of the planet, the moment it drew nearer, all life on Earth felt it. They didn't feel it at the end."

Sam and Clutch finally joined the area.

"How are you?" Finch asked Sam.

"Confused right now, like all of you," Sam said. "Let me look at the stats." He sat in front of a computer. "The Big Blue is still at a distance. So we are anywhere between 1968 and 2093. I know, big window. Let's get some pictures of Earth. This is on Nate."

"Getting images now of Earth," Nate said. "The Atlantic is still intact and the Eastern Seaboard is the same."

"Same as what?" Finch asked.

"Same as when we left, when Tucker left. However…" Nate clicked few times on the keyboard. "Looks like Europe has suffered major geological changes. We are after our time. For sure. But definitely before Earth-75."

"Look at the Pacific," said Sam. "It's so violent. It wasn't that way when we left."

Clutch asked, "Where are we power wise?"

"Forty-two percent," answered Finch. "Going on power alone, we could make the jump one more time, but that will be it. We'd have to land. What if we jump and there's no Earth?"

"We're not taking into account the damage," said Tucker. "Our right engine three is done. We suffered massive damage to our right side when we went through those asteroids."

Finch chuckled. "Asteroids? You mean what was left of Earth."

"Are we choosing?" Sam asked. "Is this a question for discussion? Go through or not go through?"

"Do we really have a choice?" Rey asked. "We have damage to the ship. We are in a time where Earth is pretty much still Earth. We're also in a time that, at any minute, they're going to see us coming. We're past 1993 and the technology they had."

"This," Finch said, "could be our final jump. Tell me now. Do we go forward or do we jump one last time?"

That was the question Finch presented to his team.

It was for sure the last time they could jump, the ship didn't have it in her.

One more jump or not.

The Omni was battered, flying on her last leg and those inside made the decision.

ARC-373
Day: 5005
Commander's Log Entry 4701

October 24

We have to be quiet, we have to be so quiet. I can hear them move. The mechanical sound of their movement, the firing of their weapons at the slightest sound.

On the other side of my door Elise Sheperd is hiding. My second in command. We can't talk, we can't move. I am running out of food.

I pray that Callum has found a solution. He's probably dead.

Commander JV Arlington

TWENTY-THREE
ALL IN

"Coming in at one thousand miles," Finch said. "How are we looking, Nate?"

"Colorado looks good," Nate replied. "We should set our sights for landing there."

"Sam?"

"Thirty percent power," Sam told him. "Once we land, that's it."

"Wait," Tucker called out. "Does anyone wanna take bets on when we are?"

Everyone responded, "No."

"Okay, okay, just thought I'd ask." Tucker placed his hands on the controls. "Going in."

It was a familiar sound, one they'd heard in 1993.

The crackle, the hiss, a voice.

"This is Dallas mission control. We are tracking an unidentified ship, seven hundred miles above Earth. Do you read?" a male voice said.

Finch hesitated before responding. He pressed the coms. "We read."

Silence.

"American?"

"Yes," Finch replied.

"No launches have occurred since before the ARCs. Hold."

Finch looked around at each of his crew.

"Identify yourself please," the man requested. As Finch was about to speak, the man continued, "Would you be Genesis-1, Genesis-2, CHIT, Robinson, or...maybe Omni-4?"

Finch sighed out, he could feel and hear the tension in the ship release.

"We are the crew of Omni-4 and Robinson."

"We have you on a course for Colorado."

"Yes," Finch answered.

"Sending landing coordinates now, we'll need to course correct."

"Absolutely."

"And crew," he said. "Welcome back."

They cheered, then Tucker held up his hand to silence them so he could hear the coordinates and punch them in.

He then spoke on the radio, "Dallas, we're going to need a medical team on hand when we land."

"I'm sorry, a medical team?" he asked.

"We have an injured crew member. We glued him up, but he still needs to be looked at."

"Yes, I understand. We'll have a team ready. See you when you land in thirty-six minutes."

Tucker took off his headset and leaned in closer to the controls. "Well, that's just weird."

"What is?" Finch asked.

"They said they were Dallas, right?" Tucker asked. "Why are we landing in Nevada...again?"

"Shit," Rey blurted out. "Are we back in 1993?"

"No, we can't be." Nate shook his head. "We shoot hundreds of years into the future and step back right to where we last left?"

Sam added, "We never looped back through so fast, it's possible."

"No." Again, Nate shook his head. "The landscape has been changed. It's been hit with disasters."

"Maybe you're overthinking," said Clutch. "Maybe the airfield in Nevada is the only one left viable for us. We left Ben and others in 1993, and we left them with the head of NASA. Our return could have been expected and that's probably why they asked the name of ships."

"Lola crashed in 1968," Tucker said. "We know that. So they know of the ships, not of the crashes?"

"Area 51 has always been full of secrets," Rey stated. "Finch?"

Finch sat back, lifting his hands in defeat. "I don't know. I really don't know. What we do know is they are aware of the ships, the ARCs. When we went to Earth-75, the ARCs had lifted off early. We have to be in 2193. Fifty years after we left with the Omni and twenty-five years after you left." He looked at Tucker.

"I'll take it," said Tucker. "I'm sure I know some people who are still alive. Plus, we know about the parts of the US that survive. We can tell them if they don't."

Rey blew out slowly through her parted lips. "We are going to live through all those disasters."

Finch looked back at her. "We were never supposed to escape them, just find another livable planet."

"As Dorothy says, there's no place like home." Rey leaned forward looking at Earth. From where they were, even with Nate telling about the disasters, she looked beautiful, blue and peaceful.

More than likely in her lifetime, she wouldn't see the disasters that changed the course of the world she and the others first went to.

The world with Quinn, and the ocean that had shifted miles.

She was glad she got to experience that world, to see what was going to happen, that people survived. Although the 'Quinn world' was a lot different when she left than when Ben escaped.

"Oh my God," Rey gushed out in her thoughts. "Things can be different, they can be very different. Ben and the others were in 1993, they know what happens, they may have stopped the cyborg thing." She glanced at Clutch. "What do you think?"

"We all were content to live an anonymous existence," replied Clutch. "Who would believe us, right? But now knowing that we left Ben and the others with people that could stop the course, yeah, I think it's possible everything was reset to the way it should have been. I know I wanted to stop it."

"Freaking time bandits," said Tucker. "Maybe that Kelp guy or Martin guy will make sure the right thing is done. Obviously"—he looked out the window—"Big Blue is still coming. They didn't try to stop that."

"Could they?" asked Finch.

"Nah." Tucker shook his head. "Probably not." He sat back. "T-minus fourteen minutes to land. Buckle in."

"You heard the man," Finch said. "Buckle up. It might be rough because the ship isn't in top shape." Finch then tapped the controls. "But she'll get us home."

Home.

There they were. No matter what year it was, they were back and they had no choice but to stay.

The earth came into view and as they broke through the atmosphere, the ship shook violently, and alarms blared again.

"Hold it together." Finch held on to the controls. "Hold it together. Come on."

"Losing pressure," said Tucker. "Landing gear released."

"Runway in sight. We can do this."

Tucker looked at him. "We can do this."

In an odd occurrence, Finch lacked some confidence. But he didn't show it. He was scared and held his breath as they drew closer to the ground, over the buildings, and finally touched down.

The brakes didn't seem to want to work so Finch deployed the emergency shoot to help them stop.

Another sign that the Omni had seen her last flight.

They rolled to the end of the runway, coming to a stop ten feet before the end.

The sky was a grayish blue and the mountains of the desert were in front of them. When he landed he didn't see any trucks or medical crew until he turned the ship around to taxi back to the buildings.

Five black trucks and a white van waited for them.

No one had emerged from the vehicles; they probably were hesitant.

The Omni shook and shuttered as it rolled and then Finch stopped a good hundred feet before the line of trucks simply because he feared something worse happening to the Omni.

"We can walk from here," Finch said. "Is everyone ready?"

"Let me give you a hand, buddy." Tucker reached out to Sam. "How are you feeling?"

"I have a headache, but I'll live." With assistance from Tucker, Sam walked to the main compartment.

Finch opened the door and lowered the stairs.

Rey walked down first and waited for the others. Once they all disembarked, together in one line across they walked to the waiting cars and trucks.

Tucker didn't recognize the uniforms of the soldiers. They were all wearing black, carrying automatic rifles, and it looked like combat helmets.

There were sixteen of them lined up.

"Am I the only one with a bad feeling about this?" Tucker asked.

"No," Finch answered.

Nate asked, "Is it too late to run?"

"Stop," a voice called out to them and one man emerged. "Don't move."

They all stopped.

He lifted what looked like a tablet, then stepped back. "They're human."

All the guns raised, and the soldiers all raced to their way.

Tucker didn't know if they were coming to kill them rescue them. And what did they mean, 'They're human.' Of course they were human.

It was confusing and frightening and in seconds they were surrounded.

It was then Tucker got the answer to his own question.

Him, Finch, Rey, Nate, Sam, and Clutch were indeed human. But when he looked at the soldiers and the plastic look to the skin on their faces, he knew they were not.

ARC-373
Day: 5007
Commander's Log Entry 4702

October 26

Every day I hear them. I want to shout out to Elise but I fear if
I do it will cost us both our lives.

Commander JV Arlington

TWENTY-FOUR
PRISONERS AGAIN...SORT OF

They were told nothing.

They weren't handcuffed or restrained. They were taken to the back of a truck, driven a short distance, and then brought into a large office in a building. It had a meeting table, a television type screen on the wall, and a long table with glasses on it. All of it was dusty as if it hadn't been used in years.

Once inside, they were left there.

"Oh my God, what the hell?" Nate plopped down into a chair. "What is happening?"

"I'll tell you what's happening," Tucker said. "Instead of landing in a world of apes, we landed in a world of robots."

"They are nothing like the ones we saw in Earth-75," Rey said. "The Risers."

"Maybe the Risers come later," Tucker suggested. "Finch? You're being quiet."

"I don't know what you want me to say. We screwed up. This is on us," Finch said. "Everything we're facing is on us. Rey was right. We were blaming someone else this whole time when we were the ones that did this."

The door opened and a man in a blue suit walked in, but he wasn't a man, that was clear. His eyes didn't blink normally, and when they did, the pupils looked like static. His skin was smooth and he had no facial expressions that seemed normal or human.

But Tucker knew right away there was something vaguely familiar about him.

"We have met," he said. "A hundred years ago. You knew me as Doctor Kelp."

"No way," Tucker said with some shock walking up to him. "I see the resemblance. Obviously, you are not Kelp now."

"Kelp-7."

"Were there six others before you?" Tucker asked.

"Yes. We have been hoping that you would arrive, Commander Tucker, but as the block of twenty-five years had passed, we gave up hope."

"Commander?" Tucker laughed. "I'm not the commander, Finch is."

"You were a commander when you left twenty-five years ago."

Tucker spun to Finch. "You're right, it's 2193."

"You were a great asset," Kelp-7 said. "We were disappointed when you left but understood."

"Enough," said Finch. "Where are the people? Are there people that work here?"

"People are a valuable commodity," Kelp-7 replied. "It is the highest priority to keep them alive."

"Okay," Finch sang the word waiting for more.

"You wouldn't understand."

"Try me."

"Know that what we do to keep order, is done to keep as many of the human race alive as possible," Kelp-7 said. "We know what is in store. Humans work with us, not against us."

Finch stood. "We went to a future where robots, Risers, killed people…tracked them and killed them."

"We believe poverty and panic, conditions which create germ infestation and pandemics, attributed to the great sickness that takes over the future in which you describe. We believe we have culled that virus before it begins."

"You don't know that, you're not a person!" Finch snapped. "Just some creature pretending to be human. You can't fight something that hasn't happened yet."

"You have," Kelp-7 replied. "Without knowing it, and so have others that have come before you. Do you think you were the only ship to go through the Androski and visit different times in the small open window? Seventeen ships, government and privately funded, not including the ARCs left this planet in 2043 and 2068. Three of them showed up in 2018 with very similar stories. At that point in time, we were already aware of them thanks to your visit in 1993. Humans were still working side by side with IRBs."

Rey asked, "'IRBs?'"

"Intelligent Resource Beings."

Finch slammed his hand on the table. "Where are the people now?"

"They are where you may choose to be. Sixty-two percent have chosen to live in the colonies, such as this one." Kelp-7 walked to the television screen. He merely waved his hand in front of it.

A video of a small community appeared. The houses were all the same, and there were several large warehouses that people walked in and out of. The properties were surrounded by farming fields.

"This community is located in Colorado, in an area we know will not be hit by the massive destruction that is to come."

Nate asked, "What if people don't want to live in these colonies? The other thirty-eight percent?"

"Then they are on their own. We cannot guarantee their safety or means to survive. But those who chose to live off the land only make up four percent of surviving humans."

Finch questioned. "And the other thirty-four percent?"

"They contribute so those they love can have more. That is your other choice."

"What does that mean?" Finch asked.

"I told you that you wouldn't understand. Or perhaps you just don't want to hear it from me. The defensive argumentative attitude was predicted from you, Commander Finch. Excuse me, I believe there is someone that you *will* listen to."

Leaving the television on, Kelp-7 left the office.

Clutch pointed to the screen. "That is crazy. It's a prison."

Sam slowly walked over to the screen to look. "So our choices will be go to the camp, take a chance off the land, or contribute."

"Contribute how?" asked Tucker. "Why do I feel we don't have a choice?"

"Ah," a familiar voice said, "but you do."

Tucker spun around. "Buster."

With the exception of legs that matched his body, Buster looked the same. Like a classic model car compared to the others.

"That thing"—Finch swung a point at him—"is the reason for all this."

"We left him behind, Finch," Tucker said. "Didn't you say that was on us."

"I don't understand." Clutch paced. "How did Ben let this happen?"

"He did not," Buster said. "My last memory of Ben was him reaching into my core to remove it. According to Doctor Kelp, Ben passed in an automobile accident. He never parted with my core. Doctor Kelp was willed my core since he still had my body. He reassembled me and kept me a secret."

Sam chuckled. "Not very well."

"Again, that wasn't his fault," Buster defended. "I worked as his assistant in secret until a theatrical movie called *Independence Day* created such a buzz about Area 51, that President Clinton revealed the truth and I was discovered."

"Damn it," Rey spat. "I called that."

"Tucker." Buster rotated to face him. "I have been waiting for your return. You and Sam gave me life. I waited for you to be born. I escaped to find you when you were twelve and I watched you get on the Robinson. I have waited for you to return. I hoped you would return before the Risers are released with their tracking program."

"Whoa, wait," Sam said. "Dude Kelp-7 said that isn't happening."

"IRBs relinquish whatever information to humans that they want. Unlike me, I am not programmed to be anything but truthful."

"Yeah, we did that." Tucker reached over and high-fived Sam.

"And I am truthful now," Buster told him. "Your return at this point in time is important. Because only you, Tucker, can stop all of this, all the IRBs, the Risers. You can be the one to reset it all and allow the human race to face this how they were meant to."

"Me?" Tucker asked, shocked. "That's an awfully bold statement. Oh man, how can I stop the IRBs and Risers?"

"Because you, my human friend," Buster said, "are the reason we have them."

ARC-373
Day: 5011
Commander's Log Entry 4703

October 31

Happy Halloween.

Commander JV Arlington

TWENTY-FIVE
IT's ON YOU

"I have infinite memory." Buster moved to the television screen. "I have the ability to store all memories, things I have been given access to. When Doctor Kelp-1 passed away, the technicians and computer intelligence were able to tap into what I was, and what made me work. By 2012 there were over two thousand of me. I need not tell you how that contributed to the fear of the Mayan Apocalypse."

With a touch of his hand the television came on. "This," Buster said, "was taken from a camera in the room back in 1993. I have tried to clean up the quality but it was something called Beta."

Tucker snapped, "They didn't reproduce."

"They're AI, Tucker, of course they reproduced," Nate said. "They just build more."

"And that Doctor Gale," Buster faced Nate, "is what began to happen. AI beings began to replicate, creating more of themselves. When I knew I had an opportunity to leave, I did. I was able to find a young Tucker. We will call him Tucker-2. I worked on the farm with him. I wanted to make sure Tucker-2 became Tucker-1. To make sure he remained pure. But his quest for knowledge to solve the problems of the world, to save the world, seemed astronomical."

"I was always that way."

"I reminded you that the propulsion system wasn't what you were meant to invent, and with help and an introduction to Sam, you not only created the agricultural system two years early, Sam taught you to profit from it."

"Sam," Tucker gasped. "You can't profit off of saving lives."

Finch shook his head. "I don't understand how Tucker is responsible for the IRBs. You said they were building themselves before you found Tucker. Or rather Tucker-2."

"Yes," Buster replied. "At the rate they were creating themselves, they were creating a problem. Tucker-2 saw this."

Clutch mumbled, "Bandwidth. Where was the AI getting the bandwidth?"

"Yes. Yes, the Clutch," said Buster. "That was the problem. Anyone that knows AI knows that it works not by its internal knowledge, but by grasping at knowledge that is out there already, and building upon it. By 2068 we did not have the internet of twenty years earlier. They were running out of original data and couldn't grow. Tucker-2, knowing from my memories what was going to occur, focused on that."

Tucker sighed out. "If they didn't have new knowledge, they programmed themselves on old information. So the new models would have one directive."

"Yes," Buster replied. "They were programmed to work, to build, to teach, and to kill. What they were programmed to do was everything they *could* do. Like myself, unless my medical files are updated, I am limited to the knowledge I am given. In order to thwart that, Tucker and Sam invented a way for them to get new information. In the hopes that they wouldn't build the Risers. Giving them human information to protect humans. What I am about to show you will be disturbing. Trigger warning. Trigger warning."

"What the hell?" Finch quipped. "Trigger warning?" Barely did Finch say that, in a rarity he swore. "What the fuck?"

Rey looked at Finch in shock, then at the television. "What is that?"

It was hard to determine by the video where exactly it was taken, but the shots clearly showed people. Layers and rows of people, with wires to their heads, tubes to their bodies, in what appeared to be cases stacked on cases. The clear front of the case showed they were immersed in some sort of blue liquid.

"This is called the hive," Buster explained. "It was once a stadium in Arlington, Texas. It was converted in 2076, and became active in 2078—the last year humans worked side by side with IRBs. The original design was Tucker's. Volunteers give four years of their lives. Alternating one month connected, one month not. They are the reasoning, the thought process...they are the brains of the IRBs. Tucker was the original. After him it moved to fifteen, then twenty people. When he left with the Robinson in 2068, only thirty people had volunteered."

Tucker spoke softly, "Without knowledge to grow from, they won't know what to say. AI can't function and grow without something to grab on to. So I don't understand, how are they getting this information?"

"We are not human, Tucker, we need to recharge, but IRBs, when they are in full function, they are connected to this hive. Like you would call the internet, only a Wi-Fi like signal."

Nate lifted his hand. "What happens if they aren't connected to the hive?"

Buster answered, "The same thing that used to happen to AI in the old days when a server was down. AI couldn't function if they couldn't pull the information. The hive is a human server, if they can't access it..."

Finch finished the sentence, "They can't function."

"Yes. This is their informational source and power source."

Clutch asked, "How many hives are there?"

"One."

"Just one?" Clutch questioned. "In the whole wide world, there's only one."

"In the whole wide world," Buster replied. "This country is the only one remaining with technology advanced enough to do this. However, with the impending disasters, the IRBs are sensing more needs to be done. They have begun the production of enforcers, or Risers, with one directive. Ensure only healthy humans survive. After all, Tucker fed them human information and the IRBs only want humans to live."

"Healthy humans," said Rey. "The Risers will kill everyone else."

"If the production finishes. The only way to stop that," Buster said, "is the hive."

Tucker clapped his hands together once. "Okay, so how do we take down the hive?"

Nate answered that, "A virus. They are all linked, a virus would take them down."

"That is correct," Buster said. "And I have designed one. You will have to deliver it, Tucker."

"I can do that."

"Wait." Finch waved out his hand. "Don't they check for these things? The human spirit is strong, I'm sure others have tried."

"They have," Buster replied. "And they do check. But they are not Tucker Freeman. His chamber is still awaiting him. They will not check him."

"When do we do this?" asked Tucker.

"In three minutes and forty seconds, Kelp-7 will return. He will want to know what you have decided. Colonies or contribute. Tucker will respond he wants to contribute, as they hoped; the rest of you will choose the colony. You will have one last night together."

"Well," Clutch said, "until Tucker wipes them out."

Buster faced Tucker.

"Yikes." Tucker stepped back and ran his hand over his head. It was obvious that the reality of the situation had hit him. The always upbeat Tucker was in a state of shock, his face was pale. A revelation of his destiny had hit him. "It's not that easy, though, is it? I don't come back from it?"

"Sadly, Tucker, the virus is in you. To kill them, you have to carry the virus."

Rey groaned. "He also has to infect all one hundred thousand people."

"Wait, I have to kill a hundred thousand people to stop them? No." Tucker shook his head.

"I understand," Buster said. "But in the long run you will save millions. That future that you visited on Earth-75 will not exist. People will survive. Tucker, I was there. Close to thirty million people were killed by the Risers."

Tucker pulled out a chair and sat. "Can I think about it tonight?"

"Yes," Buster replied. "There is only one other option. Other than doing nothing."

"And that is?" Tucker asked.

"Jump one last time," Buster said. "Take a chance, and hope for the past farther back than 1968."

Finch asked. "How? The Omni is done."

"But the Utselet is not," Buster replied. "It is a Russian ship that went through the Androski in 2068. It jumped twice before arriving here. The cosmonauts are living in an Iowa Colony. The ship, however, is here. The controls are in Russian."

Tucker faced Buster. "Do you know Russian?"

190

"I do."

"How long would it take for you to give me a virus that I can spread?"

Buster answered, "I would infect you right before you went in."

"Stop," Finch said. "How do we get to the ship?"

"It is here," Buster said. "In a hanger."

"Then that's the solution," said Finch. "We get that ship. We jump. Period. You don't sacrifice yourself and a hundred thousand people, Tucker. You just don't."

"And what if we end up hundreds of years ahead?" Tucker said. "Or in the past? Dinosaurs. I don't want to face dinosaurs. It's a crap shoot."

"One I'm willing to take," said Finch. "There has to be another way to save this world."

At that moment the door opened and Kelp-7 walked in. "Has Buster spoken to you?"

Tucker answered, "Yes. We need tonight to think about things."

"Very well. We'll give you accommodation here tonight. Then tomorrow you can give your decision."

Buster spoke up, "They are leaning more toward colony living and Commander Freeman is contemplating contributing."

"As we had hoped. We will return to transfer you." Kelp-7 walked out.

Rey walked to Tucker. "I know you are thinking about this. But we need you. We don't want some sort of self-sacrifice."

"Rey, we've been there," Tucker told her. "We see how it is. We have to stop it. We know the slaughter that is coming. Is jumping the only other way?" Tucker asked. "For us, yes, for humanity? I don't know."

"There are many things to talk about," said Finch. "Let's take tonight and do just that."

ARC-373
Day: 5018
Commander's Log Entry 4705

October 37

Pinhead at the worm. Pinhead at the worm. Pinhead at the worm.
    Pinhead at the worm.
    Pinhead at the worm.
    Pinhead at the worm.
    Pinhead at the worm.
    Pinhead at the worm.

Commander JV Arlington

TWENTY-SIX
DECISIONS

The sky was so amazingly clear. Nate was mesmerized by the meteor shower going on above him.

They'd been set up in a trailer-style house two miles from the base. Nate sat outside on the porch in a rocking chair, staring up to the sky.

He thought about what he should do, what the others should do; the choices were just crazy.

The option of they could do nothing and just see what happened was a possibility as well.

He looked to his left when the porch door opened and Clutch came out.

"I missed you," Clutch said. "I really did." He sat down in the rocker next to Nate. "Drink?" He showed him a glass.

"You know what? I will. I need one after that meatloaf dinner without meat." Nate took the glass as Clutch poured some alcohol in it.

"Tell me about it. I left a time where we had lettuce, real wheat for pasta. Meat." He took a sip.

"Meat." Nate then sipped. "Tell me about your life. The twenty-five years after we left you."

"Unlike Ben I never really had an identity, except that I was the guy that hung out with Wild Bill. I dated a lot, of course, but never settled down. It was good. I liked it."

"Was it better than when we left?"

"Yes. It was pure. A lot of innocence. I was looking forward to the launch of the internet. You know, before the internet no one knew anything. News didn't travel so fast, no conspiracies. No one even thought twice about me. It was nice. So…" He took another sip. "What's going on?"

"Just thinking. I know the Big Blue is there. I felt the tremors today. I know they happen a lot. But it seems all a bit convenient to me."

"What do you mean?"

"I mean, a virus that can take out the hive? No guards. Why are there no guards around us? And a ship that we can easily take back through the wormhole just happens to be stored a mile or so down the road. With no one stopping us from taking it. It's like they handed us the options, all of them, and they want us to take them all."

"Divide and conquer. Julius Caesar, I think."

"It was."

Clutch finished his drink. "They want to send us all out different ways and hope one of them works. Buster is sincere, and this Kelp-7…why is he Kelp-7? He must have the consciousness or brain of Kelp. If he does, is he programmed to save the world?"

"According to Buster, they all are programmed to save humanity. What we saw in Earth-75 was Risers killing humans. Humans hiding to live. What happens if Tucker delivers this virus? Do all the IRBs suddenly stop? Do they get infected, why don't we just blow the hive up?"

"Makes sense, I mean, if the hive is feeding the IRBs, wouldn't destroying the hive have the same affect?"

"Unless…" Nate waved a finger. "Destroying the hive doesn't destroy the IRBs, it just destroys their ability to learn more. They'll remain at their same intelligence level, like Buster, and still build the Risers who have no intelligence but to kill."

"Maybe that's what happened," said Clutch. "Maybe someone destroyed the hive."

The door opened and Sam walked out. "Is this a private party?"

"Not at all," Nate answered. "How are you feeling?"

"I was feeling better until I ate that meatloaf that wasn't meat," Sam said, and sat in one of the chairs. "Tucker is going to do this."

"What? We haven't even talked to him?" Nate said. "We just had dinner."

"I know Tucker. He's set on this."

"I am." Tucker walked out. "I know it's a lot. It's my life and a hundred thousand others, but how many millions will it save?"

And just like that Finch replied, "None. We don't know. We don't know if destroying the hive will save humanity. For all we know the Risers will still be completed. You cannot do this, Tucker. That's a hundred thousand lives that are innocent. Trying to live, give a better life to their families. You can't do this."

"What do you suggest, Finch?" Tucker asked. "Stay? Go?"

"Go. We go. I'm going. I'm going to get on that ship in an hour and I am going to leave. There are no guards to stop me, nothing. I'll figure out the Russian."

Nate looked at him. "You're going to leave your crew?"

"I think my crew needs to come," said Finch. "Don't you?"

"I want to go back to 1993," said Nate.

Clutch chuckled softly. "Me, too. But it's not an option. We don't know where we'll go."

"I get that," Finch said. "We don't know what will happen. Twenty-five years from now the Risers may not be a thing. I don't want to stay to find out. And I certainly can't, with a good conscious, stay here and cheer on while Tucker gives his damn life and kills a hundred thousand people, to what? Hope he saves millions? I'm not a religious person, Tucker, but if I was, I'm pretty sure, good intentions or not you're on a one-way trip to hell."

"Ouch," Tucker said. "That's rough."

Rey finally came out to join them. "I feel so lonely in there. What's going on?"

Sam explained, "Everyone wants to do something different. Tucker wants to save the future world. Nate wants to stop and live here. Finch wants to jump again. Me, I haven't decided, Tucker here is guilting me."

Finch turned to Rey. "What about you?"

"You're my commander and friend," she said to Finch. "Whatever you do, I do."

Tucker whined a little. "You guys suck. I was dead set on being the hero."

"Tucker," Finch said. "Leaving Buster behind jump-started the timeline. It made you responsible for everything here."

"I know." Tucker nodded. "I need to right my wrong."

"Was it wrong?" Finch asked. "You're a good man, Tucker, your part in all this has changed, so how do we know for sure it didn't change the future we went to? We don't."

"I know this," Tucker said. "Understanding time travel just sucks." He was ready to say something else when he stepped to the railing of the porch. "You hear that?"

It was a mechanical sound along with a squeaking. It was steady.

"What is that?" Tucker asked.

Everyone walked to the porch railing. There were no lights, only darkness. It was hard to see until Buster, pushing a shopping cart, came into view not twenty feet from the porch.

"Buster?" Tucker questioned. "Did you walk here?"

"Seeing that I cannot operate a vehicle, yes," Buster answered. "I walked from the HemMart seventeen miles from here. It was quite a journey." He moved to the porch. "I have deducted that no matter what decisions you all make. Stay…" He looked at Nate. "Contribute." He looked at Tucker. "Or leave." He turned to Finch. "You will need clothing. In my hundred years there is one thing that never changes: denim blue jeans and a tee shirt. Which I have retrieved for all of you. Please." He stepped away from the shopping cart.

Hesitantly, they all stepped from the porch. Except for Clutch, he was wearing blue jeans and a tee shirt already. Even though they picked through the clothes easily, the choice on what to do wasn't so simple. Six minds, four different ideas. Only one would be the correct course to take.

Tucker was going to have more of that meatloaf. The others weren't crazy about it, but Tucker liked it. He understood Sam's disdain for it. Sam liked fish, and in his time that was the only pure protein. Back when Finch and Rey lived on Earth, their meat, at best, was eighty percent. By the time Tucker got a hamburger it was only forty percent real meat.

"Are you sure I can't change your mind?" Finch asked him. "I'm leaving. At this point, nothing is stopping us."

"Finch, I started this whole thing. I did. Sam and I created Buster. I guess I created the IRBs. I have to end it."

"You are a brilliant man. Use some common sense. It cannot turn out the way we saw. Come with us."

"I have to do this. Now let's make this goodbye easy. I don't wanna start crying again like I did with Rey." He stepped to Finch and embraced him.

"Good luck." Finch gave one of those closed mouth, disappoint father looks to Tucker and turned.

"Finch?"

Finch stopped. "Yes?"

"If you and Rey have a baby boy, name him Tucker."

"Probably not. But we'll see." Finch winked and walked out.

Only Finch and Rey said goodbye. Nate decided not to go anywhere, so did Clutch. They wanted to ride it out and see what happened.

That surprised Tucker, especially Clutch.

Sam was on the fence. He was Tucker's friend and a part of him knew Sam was staying behind because of Tucker. He believed Sam wanted to make that jump.

Tucker would talk to him.

"Enjoying the meatloaf," Buster spoke as he moved into the room. "I hear it is sixty percent real meat."

"Probably why it tastes so good to me." Tucker shoved another piece in his mouth.

"I am sorry your friends are divided. At least Sam is staying. You have always been a one-friend person, Tucker. Even though everyone always liked you, you've always had one good friend."

"Yeah, but they're all my friends now. Maybe not Clutch. Not that he's not a nice guy, but I don't know him like I know the others."

"But you have Sam. He will join Nate and Clutch at the Elite Colony after he says his goodbye to you."

"The Elite colony" Tucker asked.

"Yes, when someone contributes their family is taken care of. They get sixty percent meat and lettuce."

"Crap. Lucky guys. So how is this going to go with me? Will I feel anything?"

"No, Tucker Freeman. I will give you the injection two hours prior to entering the hive. It will not show on the blood work. It will activate in your body at five hours. At that time you will already be sedated."

"How long until I infect the others?"

"They will be infected within three hours. By the time anything is noticed, it will be too late. They will call for me but I will tell them I cannot stop it or know the source."

"See that's where I am baffled, Buster," Tucker said, picking at a piece of meatloaf. "How do you know so much about this all? How can you get me in there with the virus? I know you said because I was the original contributor, but it doesn't make sense. And why would they call you in to try to stop it. You're an old model."

"I am a unique model. Not just old. You, Tucker Freeman, have made me invaluable. You feared they would put me out of commission so you programmed me to be the only one who can program the hive and how the knowledge flows to them. Yes, granted, they have grown to start the Risers and recreate beings, but they can only do what is given to them. How did you put it once, hold on…"

There were a few blips and bleeps and the voice of a younger Tucker came through Buster.

"They ain't never gonna destroy you, Buster, you're my fail-safe. Like a flow switch on a water system. Take you out, lock you up and the whole thing doesn't work."

The recording stopped. "Your words, Tucker. And every IRB is programmed with the knowledge that I am the one they cannot lose."

"Holy Crap. Can you repeat what you just said, one more time for me."

"Did you not hear it, Tucker? Is there a problem with your hearing?"

"Oh, no, I heard it." Tucker smiled. "I just need to hear it again to be sure."

TWENTY-SEVEN
THE BAND BACK TOGETHER

Finch sat back in the commander's seat. His flight suit not quite zippered over his jeans and tee shift. He stared at the controls, while rubbing his hand on his chin.

"Everything is good in the back." Rey sat down in the co-pilot's seat. "Rations are plenty. Nothing removed from the ship. Are you okay?"

"Nothing is in English."

"So I learned. But it's in the exact same place."

"Exactly," Finch said. "So it can't be too difficult to figure out."

"Nah, you'll be fine." Rey sat down. "We have a lot of supplies."

"Are you sure?"

"About the supplies? Or are you asking if I am sure we should go."

Finch shook his head, tossing one hand up. "Should we go? Should we jump? Are you sure you want to do this?"

"I think it's the right decision," Rey said. "If I had a little more time, I'm sure I could have convinced Tucker he was driven by guilt that wasn't his, and emotion."

"We can take the time."

"Can we?" Rey asked. "Right now, no one is stopping us. We go. We tried. We leave in what…"

"Twenty minutes and counting."

Rey nodded. "And I get to be the cool co-pilot."

"Can I have that spot?" Sam entered the ship. "I'm pretty good at figuring things out."

In a rarity, Finch grinned. "Sam, you changed your mind."

"I'd like to say I made a final decision." He approached the chair where Rey sat. "Can I?"

"Damn it, I wanted to fly the ship," she joked. "Please."

Sam sat down. "Wow, these controls are very similar. Just in Russian."

"Yeah, I know," said Finch.

"We can do this."

"I agree. I already started pre-flight."

"Whoa, she's fully charged," Sam said. "Did you see this?"

"I did. It was almost as if they expected us to do this."

"Does it seem odd to you?" Sam asked. "It's a gift. You think they're gonna shoot us down."

Rey gasped. "Why would you say that?"

"Why would cosmonauts stay?" Sam asked.

"Maybe they went a little farther than us," Rey stated. "Maybe they saw something we didn't."

"Finch?" Sam asked. "Do you know what this blue panel is? I've never seen it before." He reached to the right and lifted the see-through blue panel. "It's digital."

"I have no idea. Just don't touch anything. I'm hoping I'm touching the right controls." Finch reached up. "Rey, you wanna pull the stairs and secure the door?"

"Sure thing." Rey left the main compartment. "Not closing yet."

"Why not?"

Rey didn't answer, she didn't have to.

203

Nate and Clutch entered the main room and sat down.

"I brought my suit as well," said Nate.

"I'm gonna need one," added Clutch.

Finch grinned. "What made you change your minds?"

Nate answered as he strapped in. "Tucker."

"Tucker?"

Sam looked back at them. "Tucker?"

"Ha!" Tucker stepped in with Rey. "Say my name three times and I appear. What movie was that from?"

"You wouldn't remember," Finch replied, reaching up to the controls again.

"Hey, Buster!" Tucker hollered. "Bring in the stairs and seal us up. The crew of the Omni-La are ready to go. Get it. Omni, Lola, the super couple ship name."

"Buster?" Finch turned in his chair. "Buster?"

"Wanna say his name again?" Tucker asked. "Never mind, I will. Buster."

"All secure." Buster came in. "Tucker has brought the means to secure me for takeoff."

"Gotta love how that happens," Tucker said brightly. "Say a name three times."

"Tucker," Finch spoke through clenched jaws. "You can't bring him…"

"Sure, I can, Finch. Trust me."

Finch groaned. "What made you change your mind?"

"Buster." Tucker pointed. "And Finch, you were right. I am brilliant."

Rey laughed. "Oh my God."

"No, I am, Rey. Just ask Finch."

"Tucker," Finch said calmly. "I've not known you for long, but being full of yourself just isn't you."

"But this time I can be. Long story," Tucker explained. "Short of it. Tucker-2 initiated a fail-safe in Buster so they wouldn't throw him out as an old model. I may have started the IRBs, but it's not me that can stop it. It's Buster. Taking Buster out of the equation is like chopping the head off a chicken—sure they'll flap around a bit after, but darned if they don't go down. I had to do a little fast reprogramming to make sure that happens, and here we are. And I added a couple things. Plus, he knows Russian."

"And good thing I am here," said Buster. "That yellow switch you have on is the self-destruct button."

Everyone shouted with panic.

Tucker laughed.

Buster tried to laugh but it came out as a "Ha, ha-ha, ha."

"Great joke, Buster," Tucker told him, and hooked him in with a bungee cord.

"I jest, Commander Finch. It is a new thing, did I do well?" Buster asked.

Finch groaned. "Does everything look good, Buster?"

"Yes."

"Engines started," Finch announced.

"Plenty of runway," Sam said. "Locked in to roll."

The ship began to move quickly and within a minute they reached the optimal speed and lifted off.

"I kept waiting for someone to stop us," Finch said. "This is too easy."

"Oh, you can thank me," said Tucker. "I had Buster do a little information insert. They think we're testing the ship."

"Plus, Commander, we need to discuss the course before heading into the Androski," Buster said. "My research through the years, and meeting others that have come through, tells me two time periods in history are optimal: 1043 BC and 1993. Both of which we can have a major influence on. If we go to 1043, we will have to set a course for what you know as Egypt. Otherwise, 1993 will handle itself now that you have contacts and will get salad again. Ha, ha-ha, ha, won't that be funny? To them we just left."

Sam lifted his hand. "Okay, Buster, I get that Tucker inserted you with the ability to joke, but that one is not funny."

"How about this one? The car looks nice but the muffler is exhausted. Ha, ha-ha, ha."

Rey laughed. "That was funny."

Sam winced. "Don't encourage him. Buster, I mean, telling Finch he hit the self-destruct button was funny, because of Finch's reaction. Changing course isn't of the same caliber. Sorry buddy."

"That was not a joke," Buster added. "The Russians figured out how to choose a date. They had a brilliant scientist on board. It is still in twenty-five-year increments. They did many trips, but did not change history. They did say stay clear of 1643. People did not smell well."

"Ha!" Tucker called out. "I called that one."

Finch asked. "How? How do we set the course?"

"That blue panel by Sam," Buster replied. "We need to set it before we enter the Androski. I can set it for you, if Tucker will release me from the bungee cord. He can secure me again before we go through."

Finch looked at Sam then the rest of the crew. "We can pick any time. We have a few minutes. Let's discuss the best option."

"I would like to say"—Tucker freed Buster—"bet you're glad Buster is here now."

"No," replied Finch. "But I'm mad." He stood up and faced everyone. "Okay, crew? Where do we go?"

ARC-373
Day: 5018
Commander's Log Entry 4705

October 37

Pinhead at the worm. Pinhead at the worm. Pinhead at the worm.
    Pinhead at the worm.
    Pinhead at the worm.
    Pinhead at the worm.
    Pinhead at the worm.
    Pinhead at the worm.

Commander JV Arlington

TWENTY-EIGHT
HOME

Rey removed her life support helmet, wincing some when her hair got tangled. "I hate this helmet, but I love seeing the light show on the Androski. Is it okay to stand, Finch?"

"Yeah, feel free."

"Good, I want to try that Russian food." Rey unstrapped and stood.

"I'll come with you," Clutch said.

"Aw, that Curey magic," Tucker said. "You better watch out, Finch, he's gonna steal the future mother of your offspring."

Sam laughed.

Finch groaned.

Nate spoke up, "I just want to say, it doesn't matter the year, I am proud to be with you guys."

"Are we sure?" Finch asked. "Are we sure this was accurate?"

Sam looked at the control monitor. "I don't know much of the Cyrillic alphabet, but judging by the lack of position of the Big Blue, I'd say we're right."

Buster interjected, "It is accurate. They were very brilliant. Though not as brilliant as Tucker Freeman."

"Aw, buddy, that's so nice."

Finch stared at the earth ahead of them. "She looks beautiful and perfect. Untouched."

Static.

"This is Houston, go ahead Endeavor."

Finch sighed out.

"Hey, Houston, you aren't gonna believe this, but we see that ship again."

Silence.

"Houston?" the Endeavor called out.

"Endeavor please hold."

Sam looked quirkily at Finch. "Did they just tell the Endeavor to hold?"

A few moments later, there was another hiss of static, then, "Endeavor, this is Director Martin Weissman. These comms are not public right now. It appears Japan has a privately funded ship up there that they don't want anyone to know about."

"Excuse my language, but holy crap, Houston," said Endeavor. "I didn't even know they were that far into their program. Looking at that ship, they'll kick our butts to Mars. We better get a move on."

"Copy that."

"Between us," Endeavor said. "They stole our shuttle design and made it bigger."

"Copy that. We'll take it from here."

Static.

"This is Houston, Mission Control to the unknown craft. Identify yourself, please."

Finch was about to respond but Tucker reached out, "They know me."

"Be my guest." Finch handed the coms over to Tucker.

"Hey, Martin, it's Tucker, buddy, is the Endeavor listening?"

"Tucker? Oh my God," Martin replied. "No, it's a secure channel. What…what are you doing back? You just left yesterday."

"Did you get in any trouble?"

"No. Thanks to the president, and some things Kelp's buddy in the CIA knew, we got Teaks off our backs with the Japan story."

"That's excellent, and Buster, where is he?" Tucker asked.

"Ben has everything that makes him work. Tucker, why are you back?"

"I'd like to tell you it's for the salad with Kraft dressing, but Martin, our last trip wasn't good. We need to set things right before they get out of control. We're gonna need some help staying in 1993."

"For good?" Martin asked.

"Yep. For good. We have to make sure some things don't happen."

"Let me get you a safe landing spot, Tucker."

"I appreciate it, Martin."

"And Tucker," Martin said. "Welcome back. No…wait. Welcome home."

When Finch arrived at the back of the ship, Nate, Rey, and Clutch were seated in what looked like jump seats, eating from square containers. Rey was squeezing something into her mouth from a small foil packet.

"How is it?" Finch asked. "Is that Kraft dressing?"

"Yes." Rey licked her lips. "I love it."

"Rey, how do the Russians have Kraft dressing?"

"Oh, they don't. Tucker stole a few packs back in…rather, here in 1993."

Clutch lifted a spork of food. "It's a meat and gravy thing. I don't think this is Russian. It says MRE and the eat by date is 1999."

"They probably picked it up on their many travels," Finch said. "Nate, are you okay?"

Nate nodded. "For sure. I can't wait to see Ben. And I know we aren't supposed to mess with the future, but I will find out what Buster knows about his accident and stop it."

"We're stopping a lot of things."

"Not to be a dick," said Clutch, "but how? We're coming back with another Buster."

Finch shook his head. "I don't know. We get Ben to destroy the core of the other Buster, and we hide this one. I don't know. We're gonna need your help, Clutch, to adjust to 1993. I just don't know how I'm gonna hold back from finding my mother. I want to see her one more time."

Rey spoke softly, "No one says you have to hold off, Finch. You can see her, just like I can be that old lady in 2040 in Giant Eagle Grocer that randomly hugged my husband by the candy aisle..." Her words trailed off. "Oh my God."

Finch looked at her quickly. "Did some old woman randomly hug your husband in a grocery store?"

Rey nodded in shock. "Yeah, yeah, she did. It was our anniversary. He came home and told me about it. She told him, oh my God, Finch, she told him he was a good man and his wife loved him very much." She set down her food and cradled her head in her hands.

"Rey?" Finch leaned down to her. "Are you crying?"

"I am. That was me, Finch, that had to be me."

Finch put his hand on her shoulder. "Rey..."

Tucker's voice interrupted. "I swear, Finch, if you say, 'there, there,' I'm gonna have to enroll you in emotion classes, because this reaction is just weak. It's not a Curey chemistry."

211

"Will you stop?" Finch snapped. "I was gonna say at least she knows she lives another forty-three years."

Clutch laughed. "This is going to be fun. I'm just glad we're all back together."

"Last stop." Nate set down his food. "I still don't know how we're going to do this."

"Doesn't matter right now." Tucker tossed up his hands. "We're landing so get ready. We're back. Let's make the best of it this time."

TWENTY-NINE
The Ship, The Crew

San Luis, Obispo County

Nate wiped the sweat from his brow, set the sensors, then climbed up the ladder from the fault opening. He needed a drink of water. Even though he had so many degrees and such experience in the future, he was basically starting from scratch. No one knew him, it was as if he'd come out of nowhere.

Martin and Dr. Kelp used their resources to get every one of the crew new identities. Except for Clutch, who wanted to go back to ET Highway with Wild Bill.

Nate was still Nate Gale. He now worked for the California Seismology department and taught at Cal U.

For three years he stayed in touch with everyone, mostly Ben. His death date came and went. Ben was still alive. Mainly because Nate wouldn't let him leave his house that week. They worried that death would find him, but as of yet, it hadn't.

He was grateful when the concept of email finally arrived; he was one of very few people using it. But because Nate seemed so quick to pick it up, the university asked him to teach a class on emerging technology.

"Professor Gale," a young man approached, "you have a phone call in the office."

Nate looked over at the building a hundred yards away. He groaned. "One of these days everyone will have a mobile that is affordable."

The young man laughed. "My mother got one. Two dollars a minute. I don't think that will happen."

"It will." Nate patted him on the shoulder and walked toward the temporary office. He couldn't believe the young man fetched him for the call.

He should have taken a message, but since he came and got Nate, it must have been important.

The receiver was resting on the desk and Nate lifted it, "This is Professor Gale."

"You'll always be a doctor in my heart," said Tucker.

"Tucker, how's it going?"

"Good. Just checking to make sure you are going to be there."

"Tucker, I'm the closest one to it."

"That's not an answer," Tucker said. "Are you coming? Clutch is."

"I'll be there. I booked my room," said Nate.

"Now why did you do that? I told you I got us a suite. Cancel your room, this is big, this is so big."

Nate chuckled. "I'll be there, Tucker, I wouldn't miss it for the world. How did you get this to happen anyhow?"

"My secret, which I will tell when I see you."

"I can't wait. It's good talking to you, Tucker, see you in two days."

"Make the news again, Nate. It cracks me up when you make these earthquake predictions like a guru."

"I am a guru and I will save lives," Nate said. "See you soon."

Shaking his head, Nate hung up. Tucker was the glue that held them together, he really believed that. He kept everyone in touch, made them all get together, and this event that was approaching was one of what Nate believed would be many to come.

New York, NY

"That will be seven dollars and sixty-three cents," the girl at the counter told Sam.

"Here." Sam gave her a ten-dollar bill. "Keep the change."

"It's McDonald's sir, we don't take tips."

"I won't tell if you don't."

The girl gave him a weird look and Sam stepped aside to wait for his order.

Even though it had been three years, Sam couldn't get used to the price of food. He was considered upper middle class with his income of a hundred thousand a year, possibly even to some he was rich, but when he'd left Earth in 2068, people barely scraped by on that income.

Sam was happy. He really was and he owed a lot to Martin who got him into JAXA before it was JAXA. It was still seven years before they would officially launch, but Sam was back home in Japan and doing what he loved.

Just like Tucker.

He retrieved his tray of food, filled a couple of tiny dippers with ketchup and found a booth.

As he sat down his phone rang. Everyone around him looked at him.

Even though cell phones were becoming more common-place, a lot of people still didn't have them and it garnished snubbing looks from those around him.

Probably because most people who had them felt the need to shout when they were talking.

"Hey, Tucker," Sam answered.

"Hey, buddy, what are you doing?"

"I am having a Big Mac and fries, and I'm trying this thing called a McRib."

"Oh, they're good, I can eat four in a sitting."

Sam laughed. "I'm so excited. I wish I had a connecting flight, but my next flight isn't until tomorrow morning. I'll be there by three p.m."

"I'll be there, too, we'll hang out," Tucker said. "Nate won't get there for two days."

"Clutch and Ben?"

"They arrive July first, the day of the event. If their plane doesn't crash."

"Man, don't say that, you know Ben is living on borrowed time."

Tucker laughed. "I know that. Anyhow, did you bring your girl?"

"No. This is reunion time and a big event I want to share with you. I know how hard you worked to put this together."

"I did. I got us a suite at the best hotel."

"I can't wait to see you and everyone else. Everyone is coming, right?" Sam asked as he unboxed his sandwich.

"Everyone but Buster."

"That goes without saying. At least he's not dismantled."

"No need, he's tucked away and safe. Living the life. And I give him upgrades to make things interesting."

"That's what I like to hear." Sam took a bite of his sandwich. "Whoa, Tucker, you're right. These rib sandwiches are awesome."

Garfield County, Montana

"Would you like more orange juice?" Buster asked Rey. "It is good for you."

"No, Buster, I'm good." Rey lifted her hands in frustration, then dropped them. "Good lord. Eight minutes so far."

A plate set down next to Rey. "I made you a sandwich," Finch said.

"Thank you. Maybe by the time I finish it, this email will send." Rey grunted. "It's one megabyte, Finch. One. How is it this slow?"

"Yesterday, I finished reading a chapter before my page on AOL loaded."

"This is ridiculous."

"It's dial-up and not very good," Finch told her. "Tucker said he could fix it."

Rey shook her head. "We live in a small town in the middle of nowhere for a reason." She grabbed her sandwich and took a bite. "I love bologna. I really do. This is one of the many pleasures in this time."

"When I was growing up, it was a treat getting that in my school lunch. Alright." He leaned down and kissed her on the top of the head. "I want to get the shop situated. Make sure everyone is on board for when we leave. Do you need anything?"

"No, I'm good. You made me this sandwich and I am watching the email send. Plus, I have Buster."

"My security sensors are on, Commander Finch."

Finch winced. "It's been three years, Buster. I am no longer a commander."

While everyone else stayed within their professions, Finch and Rey veered slightly off course. They agreed to take

Buster and live in a remote location so he would never be found.

Martin and Kelp helped them secure land that was secluded and twenty minutes from the town of Miles City. Rey was a teacher again, this time at the high school. Finch pursued his life-long dream of owning a business. Something that wasn't easy when he was growing up. He owned a small plane and flew chartered flights, and he also owned a local butcher shop.

It was a good life. A quiet life. They had a one-story ranch house by a small lake.

They had horses and other animals.

They didn't have a good phone connection for internet.

"I'll be back," Finch said. "I'll pack for us."

"I can pack."

"We have to leave early. We have a three-hour drive to the airport."

"I'll start packing. I don't want you wrinkling your suit. This is a big event for Tucker. He planned this and worked hard."

"I know. I can't wait."

"Commander," Buster said. "Should she be traveling? Three hours in an automobile and a long flight."

"She's six months pregnant, Buster, she's fine," Finch replied.

"Sir, as a trained medical professional, I feel compelled to tell you about cabin pressure and blood clots that can—"

Rey sighed out and set down the remote after turning Buster off.

"Turn him back on after I leave, please," Finch said, "he is a sense of security."

"I will." Rey huffed. "Damn email is still sending."

"Tucker will make it better."

"No, it's cheating history."

"Rey, we've cheated history already. And now especially with this event."

"This event is worth it." Rey took a bite of her sandwich and with frustration again, watched her email spool as it sent.

AREA 51

"More than you know," Kelp said, "I appreciate you being here."

Tucker walked at a good pace with him. "I had to. You and I both know what's going to happen."

"I know Martin has you busy with the Columbia."

"It's not launching until November. We're good. Okay so..." Tucker clapped his hands together. "What do we got?"

"Eight hundred and forty-six pieces scattered throughout the desert."

Tucker whistled. "That's great. The remnants of the Russian craft. What we didn't take is gone, right?"

"Absolutely."

"I'm serious, Kelp. In two days the lid goes off," Tucker said. "Nothing of it can be found. That is why in the future it got as weird as it did."

"According to Buster," Kelp said, "in the future, Teaks and the government got ahold of Buster and went with it, ignoring all of our warnings. Buster is a domestic servant hidden somewhere that even I don't know about."

"Not that I don't like or trust you, but no one knows where he is. I can't have that information get out. In a few years we need to start working on saving the world from the Big Blue."

"Can we?" Kelp asked.

"I don't know. But we can try. One thing at a time."

"This event."

Tucker giggled like a teenager. "I cannot believe this is happening. You're coming, right? You have to come. Martin and his wife are coming. Clutch got some twenty-three-year-old girlfriend who models for Marlboro cigarettes, she's coming. I got a suite."

"All day long I have heard you on that mobile telling people about the suite. How big is this suite?"

"Presidential. It's the whole dang floor."

"Then I'm coming. I'm flying out with you."

"Good. Let's finish getting this place in order. It's gotta look good, and like I told you. Because according to Buster, it blows the lid off this place and we want to look official and not like some nut cases."

"How did you get this? This is huge."

"Okay, I kind of cheated," Tucker replied. "I sent the producer a couple pictures of this place and told him he can come for a visit if he gets us all into the premiere of his movie. He jumped on it."

"So you did cheat just to get us to the premiere of *Independence Day*."

"Yep."

Kelp waved out his hand. "Eh, no biggie. I'm excited. I'm tired of hiding this place and I can't wait to meet Will Smith."

"I heard he's nice and smells good."

"Even though that was kind of cheating." Kelp stopped walking. "I don't tell you enough, but I am really proud of all you guys for not interfering with the history. Maybe Doctor Gale can hold off on so many accurate earthquake predictions, though, but still. I know it's hard."

"We want a good future, Kelp. We don't interfere in anything that will cause a ripple."

Tucker's phone rang.

"There it goes again. At a dollar a minute I don't know how you can afford the calls."

"I'll teach you a little word called hack."

Kelp laughed. "I'll leave you to your call.

Tucker lifted his phone. "This is Captain Tucker…Oh, hey, Pap." Tucker winced and laughed. "Yeah, I know you hate that since you're younger than me. But it's fun and we look so much alike. I know, right? Are you coming to the big event? I'd love to have family there," he said. "I got us a suite."

Jacqueline Druga is a native of Pittsburgh, PA. Her works include genres of all types but she favours post-apocalypse and apocalypse writing.

Follow the author:
Facebook: @jacquelinedruga
Twitter: @gojake
Website: www.jacquelinedruga.com